# AVAILABLE NOW!

*James Patterson's*
## BOOKSHOTS
*Flames*

### LEARNING TO RIDE

City girl Madeline Harper never wanted to love a cowboy. But rodeo king Tanner Callen might change her mind...and win her heart.

### THE McCULLAGH INN IN MAINE

Chelsea O'Kane escapes to Maine to build a new life—until she runs into Jeremy Holland, an old flame....

## BOOKSHOTS

### CROSS KILL

*Along Came a Spider* killer Gary Soneji died years ago. But Alex Cross swears he sees Soneji gun down his partner. Is his greatest enemy back from the grave?

### ZOO II

Humans are evolving into a savage new species that could save civilization—or end it. James Patterson's *Zoo* was just the beginning.

## THE TRIAL: WOMEN'S MURDER CLUB

An accused killer will do anything to disrupt his own trial, including a courtroom shocker that Lindsay Boxer will never see coming.

## LITTLE BLACK DRESS

Can a little black dress change everything? What begins as one woman's fantasy is about to go too far.

# UPCOMING BOOKSHOTS FLAMES ROMANCES

## SACKING THE QUARTERBACK

Attorney Melissa St. James wins every case. Now, when she's defending football superstar Grayson Knight, her heart is on the line too.

## DAZZLING—THE DIAMOND TRILOGY, PART I

To support her artistic career, Siobhan Dempsey works at the elite Stone Room in New York City…never expecting to be swept away by Derick Miller.

## RADIANT—THE DIAMOND TRILOGY, PART II

After an explosive breakup with her billionaire boyfriend, Siobhan moves to Detroit to pursue her art. But Derick isn't ready to give her up.

## BODYGUARD

Special Agent Abbie Whitmore has only one task: protect Congressman Jonathan Lassiter from a violent cartel's threats. Yet she's never had to do it while falling in love....

# UPCOMING BOOKSHOTS THRILLERS

## LET'S PLAY MAKE-BELIEVE

Christy and Marty just met, and it's love at first sight. Or is it? One of them is playing a dangerous game—and only one will survive.

## CHASE

A man falls to his death in an apparent accident....But why does he have the fingerprints of another man who is already dead? Detective Michael Bennett is on the case.

## HUNTED

Someone is luring men from the streets to play a mysterious, high-stakes game. Former Special Forces officer David Shelley goes undercover to shut it down—but will he win?

## $10,000,000 MARRIAGE PROPOSAL

A mysterious billboard offering $10 million to get married intrigues three single women in LA. But who is Mr. Right...and is he the perfect match for the lucky winner?

## FRENCH KISS

It's hard enough to move to a new city, but now everyone French detective Luc Moncrief cares about is being killed off. Welcome to New York.

## KILLER CHEF

Caleb Rooney knows how to do two things: run a food truck and solve a murder. When people suddenly start dying of foodborne illnesses, the stakes are higher than ever....

## 113 MINUTES

Molly Rourke's son has been murdered. Now she'll do whatever it takes to get justice. No one should underestimate a mother's love....

## THE CHRISTMAS MYSTERY

Two stolen paintings disappear from a Park Avenue murder scene— French detective Luc Moncrief is in for a merry Christmas.

## BLACK & BLUE

Detective Harry Blue is determined to take down the serial killer who's abducted several women, but her mission leads to a shocking revelation.

*Her second chance at love might
be too good to be true....*

When Chelsea O'Kane escapes to her family's inn in Maine,
all she's got are fresh bruises, a gun in her lap, and a desire to
start anew. That's when she runs into her old flame, Jeremy
Holland. As he helps her fix up the inn, they rediscover what
they once loved about each other.

Until it seems too good to last…

**Read the stirring story of hope and redemption**
*The McCullagh Inn in Maine,* **available only from**

# Learning to Ride

## ERIN KNIGHTLEY

James Patterson's
BOOK**SH**TS
*Flames*

Little, Brown and Company

New York  Boston  London

Copyright © 2016 by Erin Knightley
Foreword copyright © 2016 by James Patterson

Hachette Book Group supports the right to free expression and the value of copyright. The purpose of copyright is to encourage writers and artists to produce the creative works that enrich our culture.

The scanning, uploading, and distribution of this book without permission is a theft of the author's intellectual property. If you would like permission to use material from the book (other than for review purposes), please contact permissions@hbgusa.com. Thank you for your support of the author's rights.

BookShots / Little, Brown and Company
Hachette Book Group
1290 Avenue of the Americas, New York, NY 10104
bookshots.com

First Edition: July 2016

BookShots is an imprint of Little, Brown and Company, a division of Hachette Book Group, Inc. The Little, Brown name and logo are trademarks of Hachette Book Group, Inc. The BookShots name and logo are trademarks of JBP Business, LLC.

The publisher is not responsible for websites (or their content) that are not owned by the publisher.

The Hachette Speakers Bureau provides a wide range of authors for speaking events. To find out more, go to hachettespeakersbureau.com or call (866) 376-6591.

ISBN 978-0-316-27634-4
LCCN 2016935243

10 9 8 7 6 5 4 3 2 1

RRD-C

Printed in the United States of America

When I first had the idea for BookShots, I knew that I wanted to include romantic stories. The whole point of BookShots is to give people lightning-fast reads that completely capture them for a couple hours in their day—so publishing romance felt right.

I have a lot of respect for romance authors. I took a stab at the genre when I wrote *Suzanne's Diary for Nicholas* and *Sundays at Tiffany's*. While I was happy with the results, I learned that the process of writing those stories required hard work and dedication.

That's why I wanted to pair up with the best romance authors for BookShots. I work with writers who know how to draw emotions out of their characters, all while catapulting their plots forward at breakneck speeds.

Erin Knightley is one of those authors and *Learning to Ride* is one of those stories. Here you'll meet Tanner and Madeline, two people from entirely different walks of life who find themselves taking an unlikely chance at love. Their path seems impossible, especially since Madeline is so determined to make a name for herself at her new job. I hope you enjoy their journey.

James Patterson

# Chapter 1

STARING AT THE rough-and-tumble, straight-out-of-an-eighties-movie roadhouse bar before her, Madeline Harper couldn't help but reconsider her decision to come here at all. Clearly the echoing silence of the past few days was messing with her sanity.

Neon pink and blue signs buzzed and flickered from the darkened windows at the front, proclaiming the names of several brands of beer she didn't recognize, while a larger white neon sign proudly spelled out the bar's name: THE REBEL YELL.

God help her.

At any sane point in her life, she would have turned around, gotten back into her tidy little white two-door BMW, and driven back to her motel room. She would have opened a nice bottle of wine, slipped into her favorite boutique pajamas, and gotten lost in a good book.

However, after doing exactly that every night this week inside the world's sleepiest motel in the world's quietest town, well, she needed *noise*. And people. And energy. She had no illusions about finding the same sort of beautiful, chaotic bustle she was used to back home in New York City. In a town where exactly one place of business was open past eight o'clock on a Thursday night, The Rebel Yell would have to do.

And really, it wasn't all bad. The parking lot was surprisingly full. While definitely honky-tonk-esque, the building was at least in decent repair, with fresh wooden railings lining the three steps to the door. Best of all, the lively din of music and laughter emanating from within were the first signs of real life she'd seen in a week.

People, music, drinks—not that different from a club in NYC, after all. And she *had* wanted to do Texas right, hadn't she? At least that's what she and her friends had joked about when she'd learned of her promotion and transfer to tiny Sunnybell, Texas, only weeks ago.

They had all crowed with laughter over their caramel appletinis after Aisha had declared Madeline must send pictures of the first cowboy she encountered. "Bonus points if he's wearing nothing but a cowboy hat and a smile."

She grinned now thinking about it. She wasn't the type to pick up some random cowboy—or random banker, stockbroker, or bartender, for that matter—but the memory did lighten her mood enough for her to push past her misgivings. Drawing a fortifying breath, she squared her shoulders, climbed the stairs, and pushed through the saloon-style louvered doors.

The place was dark and smoky but full of life. She scanned the room as she made her way to the bar, trying not to look like too much of a tourist. The walls were made of rough-hewn planks and covered in lassos, bridles, old pictures, and beer signs. Something told her this wasn't the replica stuff you saw on the walls of some of those chain restaurants. Just like the cowboys at the bar weren't the kind from a Hollywood set.

Everything about the place seemed genuine.

The building itself was actually pretty big, with tall tables lining one wall, pool tables along another, and a stage all the way at the back. A country-western band, complete with bolo ties, cowboy hats, and boots, belted out a rowdy dance rendition of a song she vaguely recognized.

But it was the boxing-ring-sized corral in the center of the building that really caught her eye. There, an honest-to-God mechanical bull swung back and forth, dipping and bucking as a laughing woman with big hair and tiny shorts held on for dear life. The ring was surrounded on all sides by beer-drinking spectators, all of whom were laughing and cheering her on.

"Ride 'em, Amber," a woman shouted as she bumped past Madeline with two bottles of beer. "Show that steer who's boss!"

Madeline wasn't sure if Amber was winning or losing, but her boobs sure looked great in the process, which was probably the point. *More power to her,* Madeline thought as she stopped in front of the bar. It didn't matter that the music was completely foreign or that the crowd looked like extras in a country music video—when it came to attracting the opposite sex, it seemed the mechanics were the same.

"What'll ya have, darlin'?" the bartender asked, his eyebrows raised expectantly. Though the bar was crowded, he leaned forward and grinned at her as though he had all the time in the world.

A half dozen cocktails came to mind, but the likelihood of getting one here was probably slim to none, judging by the lack of bottles behind the bar. "I think it's probably safer to ask what you're serving," she said with a wry smile.

He ticked off five different types of beer and two rotgut whiskeys. She chose a bottle of the only beer she recognized. It was sufficiently cold and tasted exactly like college. Turning, she surveyed the room again, glad to have something to do with her hands. The place really wasn't so bad. It would be fun, actually, if her friends were here to share the experience.

As it was, she leaned against the wall and hung out the Do Not Disturb sign across her forehead. She soaked in the noise, bustle, and activity, happy to have something remotely familiar in this strange place. She'd finish her drink, perhaps have another, and then maybe, *maybe* she'd strike up a conversation.

When in Rome…

Madeline Harper, Calvin Aviation Supply's newest and youngest-ever acquisitions division manager, was about to get her honky-tonk on.

\* \* \*

Tanner Callen saw her the moment she stepped foot in the joint.

*Well, well, well.* The hot-as-hell Yankee had ventured out from the motel at last. He'd seen her zipping in and out of the parking lot in her fancy Bimmer with the New York plates a few times this week, her face half covered by those dark, over-sized sunglasses of hers. But even if he hadn't seen her plates, he would have known she was an out-of-towner at first glance. Her designer jeans and red-bottomed heels stood out in the sea of worn Levi's and scuffed boots like a silk rose in a field of bluebonnets.

Her top was low-cut but loose, giving teasing hints of her trim figure as she shimmied her way to the bar and ordered a drink. Tanner shook his head; Evan looked like he was about to trip over his fool tongue as he served her a bottle of beer.

"Better take your shot or I'm callin' forfeit, Callen."

Tanner dragged his attention away from the bar and laughed at his friend Mack. "You know that's the only way you'll ever win." He and Mack had been friends since the eighth grade, and ribbing each other was part of the game.

Diego, who was a few years younger and still pretty wet be-hind the ears, chuckled and gave Mack a solid punch on the shoulder. "Burn. You gonna let him get away with that smack talk?"

Shaking his head, Mack shrugged. "He can talk all he

wants, but by the end of the night, dollars to donuts he'll be the one taking the ride of shame on old Bucky."

Tanner snorted as he set his beer down on the peanut-shell-covered table and picked up his pool cue. "Big talk, considering it was your backside getting tossed off that old bull last time. And the time before that."

It was a longstanding bet: whoever lost two out of three games on The Yell's ancient coin-operated pool tables had a date with Bucky. What better way to give a rodeo star his comeuppance than to have him thrown like a sack of potatoes from a mechanical bull?

Tanner glanced behind him one more time before turning his attention to the game. Miss New York still leaned against the bar, her honey-blond hair grazing those sexy bare shoulders of hers.

Forget Bucky—if Tanner had a date with anyone tonight, he hoped like hell it would be with that little high-heel-wearing Yankee. Lucky for him, the night had only just begun.

# Chapter 2

"CARE TO DANCE?"

Madeline flicked her gaze from the bullpen to the denim-shirt-clad guy who'd materialized at her side. This one was actually pretty cute, in a puppy dog sort of way. She still wasn't going to dance with the man—or anyone else, for that matter—but she did smile back at him. "Thanks, but no dancing for me tonight."

It was the same thing she'd said to every other guy who had asked that night. She half expected him to say something cutting—that had happened way too many times in her life—but he just tipped his hat, offered up a toothy grin, and moved on.

Amazing.

Seriously, every man should take a lesson in rejection from the cowboys in this town. She grinned as she looked down at her nearly empty beer bottle and shook her head. Apparently it had only taken two drinks to soften her up to this place. Though she'd deny it to any of her friends back home, she'd been having entirely too much fun watching the mechanical bull show. The thing seemed to have two settings: sexy boob-jiggler and insane bull-on-crack. Not surprisingly, the rider's gender seemed to determine the setting.

"When you gonna take a turn, blondie?"

Madeline looked over to find a tall brunette with a tight plaid shirt and killer jeans offering up a wide, friendly smile. She'd seen the woman ride a few minutes ago. She'd been good, actually. Madeline shrugged and flashed a wry grin. "I'll leave it to the professionals, thank you."

"We all have to start somewhere," the woman said, raising her eyebrows as further invitation. "I'm Ashley, by the way."

"Madeline," she said with a nod of greeting. "And I'm pretty sure you'll see me sprout wings and fly before you see me on that thing." Given her deathly fear of flying, that was saying something.

But before Ashley could respond, something across the room caught her attention. "Oh. My. Lord." Her eyes were wide as she turned to Madeline. "'Scuse me, darlin'. I'll be back." She rushed off toward a group of similarly dressed women who were standing at the ropes on the other side of the corral.

*Odd.* Shrugging, Madeline turned back to the main attraction. She started to lift her beer for the last swig but suddenly froze, eyes wide. Where the hell had *that* guy come from?

He stepped into the corral, sauntering despite the uneven, cushioned surface. He was the embodiment of cowboy sexy—

something she hadn't known existed until that exact moment. Tall, bearded, sure-footed, broad-shouldered, flat-ab'd, and hot enough to singe those broken-in jeans he wore so well.

And she wasn't the only one who noticed.

The atmosphere of the place seemed to change as he swung up onto the mechanical bull, a wry, self-deprecating grin tugging at one corner of his mouth. All at once, Ashley's sudden departure made sense. He seemed to command everyone's attention without even trying. The crowd pushed in as hoots and whistles drowned out whatever the guy with the microphone was saying. Not that Madeline gave a flip what he was saying. This cowboy was pure eye candy.

He pressed his hat more firmly over his brown hair, tucked his hand under the rope, and gave a single nod. The bull started slow, gently bucking and spinning in lazy circles. He shook his head and tossed a wicked grin toward the operator but never relaxed his stance.

Over the past hour, Madeline had seen many a half-drunk cowboy take his turn on the machine. No one possessed this man's controlled, oddly graceful moves. As the bull gradually gained momentum, he moved back and forth, swinging one arm over his head while the other remained firmly clasping the rope. Below the rolled-up sleeves of his plaid shirt, she could see the muscles of his forearms flexing this way and that.

She bit her lip. Clearly this man was no stranger to the gym.

She leaned forward against the ropes, ignoring the cacophony of laughter, shouts, music, and voices all around her, letting it all slide into the background of noise she loved so much.

God, he was sexy. And skilled, if one considered the ability to stay glued to a bucking machine a necessary life skill. Tonight, she kind of did. No one else had come close to holding on the way he managed to as the bull bucked, whirred, and spun. The faster it went, the more he seemed to deliberately swing his body to swallow the momentum, almost like a jockey absorbing the energy of a thundering racehorse. It was mesmerizing. Impressive.

Before she knew it, the buzzer sounded and the crowd erupted in cheers as the bull shuddered to a stop. Had he just won? Did one win in mechanical bull riding? Well, the spectators did, of course. She, at least, felt like she won every round she got to watch.

She didn't even try to pretend she wasn't staring as the cowboy jumped down and straightened to his full height. She always did have a thing for tall guys. Especially when they looked like a more rugged version of Chris Evans. Just as she was watching him with a look usually reserved for white chocolate cheesecake, he tipped back his hat, looked right at her, and grinned.

Caught!

Every last ounce of air whooshed from her lungs. He was *hot*. She tightened her grip on her bottle, sucked in a steadying breath, and actually managed to smile back. Thank God for those two beers. She suspected that a completely sober Madeline would have bolted for the door.

Completely sober Madeline didn't have near enough fun in life. Slightly tipsy Madeline planned to rectify that.

He held her gaze as he left the ring and walked toward her. His stride was confident but unhurried. He seemed to be savoring the anticipation. Madeline sure as hell was. Her heart was thundering, but she couldn't have looked away if she wanted to. Lucky for her, she most definitely did not want to.

As he closed the distance between them, she could see that his eyes were the same aqua-blue as her favorite jewelry box, and his left eyebrow was bisected by a thin white scar that made her think of one word: rakish.

Giving her a slow, lazy grin, he tipped his hat and said, "Howdy."

That word was *not* supposed to be sexy. It sure as hell had never been in the past. But now? Butterflies sprang to life in her belly as she looked up into his gorgeous eyes. Everything about him was sexy. She'd take a picture for her friends, but he had way too many clothes on…something she'd like to remedy. Her cheeks heated at the thought. No more beer for her tonight.

Pushing back her absurd urges, she smiled, trying to make it appear as if she hadn't just been thinking about what he'd look like naked. "Hi."

"Don't reckon I've seen you here before."

She'd never been a fan of Texan accents, but damn if his words weren't practically a caress. His voice was deep and clear, and the way he spoke made her think of warm honey and hot summer nights.

"Don't reckon you have," she said, cheekier than she'd be in normal life.

Her response made him chuckle, and he held out a hand. "Dance with me."

She'd promised herself she wouldn't dance tonight, no matter how many drinks she had. The plan had been to come, soak up the energy, observe the townspeople in their natural habitat, and return to the dreaded motel room as anonymously as when she'd left it.

But then again, she'd also once promised herself never to leave New York. Sometimes plans called for a detour or two.

Taking a deep breath, she smiled, set down her beer bottle, and slipped her hand in his.

## Chapter 3

AS HIS FINGERS closed around Madeline's, the sensation of his calloused palms abrading her own soft hands and regularly manicured nails made her shiver in the best possible way. *Hellooo, Mr. Cowboy.* She bit her lip to hold back a giggle and allowed him to lead the way to the dance floor.

Talk about surreal. It was hard to believe any of this was actually happening. Willingly dancing to country music in a Texas honky-tonk was about as far outside her box as she could get. But maybe that was why it was so oddly thrilling? Probably. Or maybe it was the man whose hand was clasped around her own, pulling her along with a confidence that he seemed to be born with.

It was a very nice view, walking behind him like this.

She'd always preferred the kind of guy who wore well-tailored suits and handsome shoes, and who exercised on a treadmill in moisture-wicking athletic wear while watching CNN or listening to his iPod. At that moment, it was hard to remember why she'd thought the *GQ* look was more attractive than a pair of Levi's that fit perfectly and a plaid shirt that was soft and faded from countless washings.

She allowed her gaze to steal over the cowboy's broad shoulders and muscled back as he cut through the crowd. This was a man who wore boots for a reason. Someone whose muscles were formed from rolling up his sleeves and doing real labor. A man who took the bull by the horns—probably literally, she thought with a stifled grin.

Tipsy Madeline had *much* better taste in men, if she did say so herself.

When they reached the farthest, darkest corner of the place, he turned and pulled her into his arms, a lazy smile lifting the corner of his mouth. There was no awkward moment of trying to find the right position; they fit together as though they'd danced a dozen times before. She let out a blissful sigh, not even caring that the music could only be described as twangy and the clientele as less than urbane. She was having fun. This was so much better than how she'd pictured her night going.

As they began to sway in time with the rhythm, he ran a hand down the back of her bare arm, his touch feather-light. "You're not from around here, are you," he drawled, though it was more of an observation than a question.

She grinned wide. "What gave me away?" she asked teasingly. She couldn't have been more obviously from out of town than if she had her New York license taped to her shirt.

He chuckled softly and pulled her in just a little bit closer. "Call it a hunch. I'll do my best to make you feel welcome."

That telltale spark of attraction ignited deep in her belly. Savoring the sensation, she tucked herself against the hard wall of his chest. "I'd say you're doing a pretty good job so far."

They moved together, their faces just a little too close, their dancing just shy of too familiar. God, she already wanted him. Really, really badly. It was more than those kissable lips she couldn't seem to take her eyes off; it was the undeniable chemistry that had sizzled between them the moment their eyes first met. Even now, she could practically feel it.

When was the last time she'd felt like this? Light and happy, intoxicated by much more than just some beer. Part of her wanted to stand on tiptoe and kiss him right then and there, but the bigger part of her wanted to savor the delicious tension building between them.

And it definitely built. After only a handful of songs, she was breathless with it. Her hands had found their way to the back of his neck, and she kept imagining pulling his head down the scant inches it would take to press her lips to his. The way he was leaning in close to her, it seemed he was imagining the same thing.

"What brought you here tonight, all by your lonesome?" he murmured, as an old classic from the fifties slid into a song she remembered hearing from the late nineties. They kept dancing, their movements languid and unhurried.

"Curiosity, I guess. Lack of options," she added with a hint of a wry grin.

"Curiosity is a good thing, and I suppose I should be grateful for the lack of options. It certainly worked in my favor tonight."

She gave a soft laugh before resting her head against his shoulder. "Mine, too." The words were almost to herself, but she knew that he had heard her when he slid his arms around her completely.

They danced that way through both slow and fast songs, tucked up against each other like lovers. When they spoke, it was with hushed voices and heads tilted together, but for the most part, they just danced.

She hadn't realized how much she had needed this. After months of working like a crazy person, trying to prepare for both the merger and her unexpected move, she hardly remembered what it felt like to relax. But here in his arms, she felt the tension melting from her body, along with all of her worries for the coming days.

She had no idea how long they'd been on the dance floor when he leaned down so his lips nearly brushed her ear. "What would you say," he asked, speaking low and slow, his warm breath caressing her neck, "if I said I wanted to kiss you, right here on the dance floor?"

A thrill raced through her as she tilted her head back to meet his warm gaze. It was heady, feeling both wanted and respected at the same time. He was giving her the chance to call the shots, while letting her know exactly what he hoped she'd say. With her heart pounding crazy hard in her ears, she lifted an eyebrow and said, "I'd say, what are you waiting for?"

His smile was sweet and devilish all at once. Still swaying to the music, he raised one hand to cup the side of her face and lowered his mouth to hers. When their lips met at last, she felt it all the way to her toes. It had definitely been worth the wait. His lips were soft but insistent, and he drew her body more firmly against his as he dipped his tongue into her mouth.

*Heaven.* She followed his lead, matching his every move with one of her own. He slanted his lips fully across her, and a breathy little moan that escaped her made him deepen the kiss more.

All the people and bustle of the room around them faded away, and it was just the two of them, lost in the moment. In the dim recesses of her mind, she realized that none of this would have ever happened in her normal life. For the first time since receiving word of her relocation, she was damn glad she'd ended up right where she was.

Damn, the woman could kiss.

Tanner would have happily kept on kissing her through the whole song if someone hadn't brushed by his back, reminding him of the audience they had all around them. Reluctantly, he drew back. Her little sound of protest went straight through him. He nearly threw caution to the wind and kissed her all over again, but he forced himself to resist.

Actually, he hadn't intended to kiss her quite so thoroughly the first time, but, well, he couldn't help himself. She was sexy as hell, and his body hummed with awareness the entire time they moved together. Some people just plain fit, and they were like two pieces of a jigsaw puzzle.

But kissing like that was bound to catch notice sooner or later, and Tanner really didn't want an audience. Instead, he tucked a lock of her silky blond hair behind her ear, letting his fingers trail down the side of her neck. "Care to move this dance somewhere a little more private?"

He hadn't been able to keep his hands off her since the moment she'd slipped her fingers in his, and the idea of having full access to her had his heart kicking against his chest like a riled bronco.

Those same fingers were now sliding their way down his back, sending all kinds of sensations through him. "Have somewhere specific in mind?"

A dozen very specific images came to mind, and none of them involved spectators. "Anywhere but here, darlin'."

She was the outsider here. He wanted the decision to be in her hands. He wanted a *lot* of things to be in her hands….

"In that case," she said, her voice low and sultry as she hooked her fingers around his belt loops, "I think I know just the place."

He couldn't resist tipping her chin up and stealing one more quick kiss. It was hot and searing, and full of promise. A night with this girl was bound to be memorable. Pulling back, he offered up a slow, intimate smile. "By all means, lead the way."

This was crazy.

*She* was crazy. Madeline had just invited a Grade-A cowboy back to her motel room, for heaven's sake! And she couldn't even blame it on the alcohol. Dancing half the night away did wonders for sobering a woman up, but in her defense, she was pretty sure it was possible to be drunk on a man's charms.

His many, many charms. She stole a look over at his muscled, denim-clad thighs as she shifted gears. No wonder he'd stayed on the bull so long. And no wonder she wasn't feeling even a hint of guilt for taking him home with her. She bit her lip. *Doing Texas right* was taking on a whole new meaning.

The motel was only half a mile away, though with her thundering pulse and fluttering nerves, it seemed much longer. Up until that moment, she'd hated the drive-up style of the place, where you could park right outside your door. Now, she was seeing the error of her ways.

It was only six steps from the car to her room. As she slipped the key into her door, he kissed the back of her neck, sending chills racing across her whole body. She shivered at the sensation even as she leaned back against him. He was warm and solid and smelled amazing. The subtle, masculine scent of his cologne was practically intoxicating.

At last the lock gave way, and they more or less tumbled

inside. She quickly shut the door behind her, dropping her keys and purse on the ground without a second thought. When she turned around, he was there, and their lips crashed together as though neither one of them could wait another second. Two steps backward and she was pressed against the door, her hands buried in his hair as his tongue tangled with hers.

*Crazy.*

She'd never done anything like this in her life. She was a three-date-minimum kind of gal, and a serial monogamist at that. But maybe that was because she'd never kissed a ruggedly handsome, hard-bodied cowboy before. Because heaven help her, it was *incredible*.

His hands slipped over her sides and down to her hips. He squeezed gently, pulling her tightly against him even as his mouth burned a trail of kisses down the length of her neck. She sighed with pleasure, tilting her head to give him better access.

Why had she never done this before? It was the single most exhilarating, thrilling experience of her life. Every day should end with making out with a hot stranger.

He leaned down, grabbed her behind her legs, and lifted her from the ground. The motion was absolutely effortless, as though she weighed no more than an empty suitcase. Four steps and they were on the bed, his warm, muscled body covering hers. God, the man could kiss. She gave herself over to his capable lips, reveling in the sensation that washed over her with each and every flick of his tongue, loving the soft scratch of his beard against her skin.

He pulled back, and she almost groaned in disappointment until he grabbed the bottom of his shirt and tugged it off. *Oh yes, much better.*

"I saw you the moment you walked in tonight," he said as his hands found the little mother-of-pearl buttons on the front of her shirt and got to work.

"You did?"

He nodded, pushing both sides of her shirt away and exposing her black lace bra. "I've had my eyes on you all night."

She shivered, as much from his appreciative blue gaze as from the cool air against her newly bared skin. "I don't know how I could have missed you." She had to have been half blind not to have seen him.

He shrugged, a teasing smile tugging at the corner of his mouth. "An oversight, I imagine," he said lightly, teasing her with his words as much as with his deliciously calloused fingertips. "I should be offended, but you did finally come to your senses."

She almost laughed. This was not coming to her senses. This was losing her mind. She didn't even know his name! And strangely enough, she didn't want to. Tonight was for fun. A crazy, intense, delectable night that she'd remember long after she was promoted right back to New York City in a year or so.

Sliding a finger down the center of his six-pack abs, she offered up a wicked grin full of promise. "I'll see what I can do to make it up to you."

When he captured her mouth in another kiss, she let go of all thoughts of the town, the quiet, and even the less-than-ideal motel bed. It was just the two of them and the incredible connection that made her heart pound and her mind whirl. Lucky for her, he was prepared, and by the time that foil wrapper hit the floor, she was more than ready for him.

When he finally pressed into her, she couldn't help but gasp against his lips. *Absolute perfection.* They seemed made for each other, moving with the same perfect rhythm they'd shared on the dance floor, their sweat-dampened bodies sliding against each other as the sound of their escalating breaths and her soft moans broke the quiet of the room. Had anything ever felt this good? She couldn't remember ever being this turned on, this attracted to anyone.

He pushed her to the edge again and again, skillfully drawing out her pleasure until at long last she shattered, crying out only seconds before he shuddered above her and collapsed, as spent as she was.

As she lay there panting for breath, reveling in the feeling of their bodies twined together, only one thought floated to the surface of her satisfaction-dazed mind:

That was one *hell* of a welcome to Sunnybell.

# Chapter 4

"GOOD MORNING, MS. HARPER. My, don't you just have a spring in your step today."

Madeline maintained her pleasantly neutral expression even as she tried valiantly to suppress the blush she could feel rising up her cheeks. She had good reason for that springy step. "Good morning, Mrs. McLeroy."

The receptionist smiled over her reading glasses as she set down her knitting. She was an odd mix of characters, with hair like Dolly Parton, a face like Mrs. Claus, and a seasonally themed wardrobe that reminded Madeline of her third grade music teacher. Today's vest featured falling autumn leaves and a smattering of friendly-looking cats.

"Mr. Westerfield said he'd like to see you once you got settled this morning." She leaned forward and added in a conspiratorial tone, "Don't you worry, though. I already plied him with coffee and my homemade banana nut muffins this morning, so I know he's as happy as a possum in a corncrib."

Madeline bit the inside of her cheek to stifle a chuckle at

the colorful comparison. She was still working on establishing her authority here and had no intention of jeopardizing it by joking around with the staff. In the week since she'd arrived, she'd been a veritable poster girl for professionalism. The older woman was sweet, but she hadn't yet realized that Madeline was soon going to be running the place, and Westerfield would be spending his days on the golf course.

Assuming this town *had* a golf course.

Nodding, Madeline thanked her before heading for her own office. As she slipped between the haphazardly arranged cubicles, she pasted a pleasant but professional smile on her face. She hoped it would disguise the barely contained giddiness she felt after one of the most amazing nights of her life. She hadn't gotten much sleep, but she still felt wired.

At six that morning, awakened by the alarm on her cell, she had feared an awkward morning-after moment. But she opened her eyes to discover that he was already gone—and she exhaled a blissful sort of sigh. No guilt, no regrets, just pure, unadulterated satisfaction. The perfect, once-in-a-lifetime encounter.

"Good morning, Ms. Harper," Kelly Ann from Sales said as she walked by, her bright pink lips stretched in an odd, almost knowing smile.

Madeline blinked. Knowing smile? No, surely not. She was just being friendly. It was hard to gauge a person's expressions when she wore a full mask of makeup this early in the morning. "Good morning," Madeline replied, her professional veneer intact.

As she walked past Geraldine's desk, the younger woman seemed to be biting back a grin. "Have a good evening?" She fluttered her lashes with over-the-top innocence.

Now that gave Madeline pause. Slowing, she said, "Yes, and I hope you did, too."

Okay, she was just being sensitive. She always had harbored an irrational fear of people somehow knowing when she had gotten lucky the night before. But then she noticed the stir around the office as, one after the other, heads popped up from behind cubicle walls like pageant-haired gophers.

Oh, no.

She walked as fast as she could the last ten feet to her office without giving the appearance of running. Or escaping. Which she was. Seriously, what did they know? She hadn't seen anyone she recognized at the bar last night. And outside of the office, no one in this town knew her yet. Even the cowboy himself hadn't known her name.

She pushed the door to her office closed and leaned against it, working to control her rising apprehension. When she was able to breathe semi-normally again, she hurried to her chair, sinking into it much the way her heart was sinking in her chest.

A brisk knock on the door made her groan out loud, but she couldn't very well ignore it. "Come in," she said, working to sound cool and collected.

Her temporary assistant, Laurie Beth, rushed inside a millisecond later, her green eyes wide and sparkling. "Lord Almighty, girl, you *must* tell me everything."

Swallowing, Madeline busied herself at her desk. "I'm not sure I know what you're referring to. Do you have the sales records I requested yesterday?"

But her assistant wasn't to be distracted. She plopped down onto the chair opposite the desk and leaned forward, eyebrows lifted. "No need to be coy, honey. You should be proud! Not a woman in this town has been able to tame Callen the Stallion, and in less than one week you managed to bring him to heel."

Callen the *what*? Madeline gaped at her, completely horrified. "What in the world are you talking about?"

"Only the fact that you took Sunnybell's most eligible bachelor home last night after a whole evening of just-this-side-of-dirty dancing." She shook her head, sending her long highlighted curls swinging. "Every female in a thirty-mile radius has wondered what it'd be like to ride Tanner's bronco. I hope you're prepared to spill some beans." She scooted forward to the edge of the chair, obviously expecting a play-by-play.

"Tanner? I thought you just said Callen?"

Laurie Beth exhaled an exasperated sigh. "Tanner Callen, rodeo star extraordinaire and all-around handsome-as-sin bachelor. Come on, Ms. Harper, I heard it from my own cousin's lips, and Amber never peddles in fibs. Her gossip is as good as gold."

Madeline was going to be sick. "And…everyone out there knows I, um, spent some time with him?"

Nodding earnestly, Laurie Beth said, "Of course! Nothing ever happens in this town, so when something like this goes down, it spreads faster than warm butter on hot bread."

Wonderful. Fantastic. Here Madeline was, doing her level best to be the professional representative from corporate that she was supposed to be, and she'd just managed to fall head-first into *Gossip Girl*.

"Laurie Beth?" she said, clinging to the tattered vestiges of her dignity.

"Ma'am?"

"Do you like working for me?" When her assistant nodded happily, Madeline looked her square in the eye. "Then let's pretend that the subject never came up, and that the people of this town have no right to my personal life. Understood?"

Laurie Beth's mouth dropped open in a neat little *O*. After a moment, she leaned back and nodded. "Yes, ma'am. You're the boss." Her good-natured shrug proved she wasn't upset by Madeline's direct comment, but something about it made her suspect Laurie Beth believed it would be just that: pretend.

The cat was officially out of the bag.

The phone rang then, cutting through Madeline's racing thoughts. "I'll call you when I need you," she said by way of dismissal before picking up the phone. She waited until her assistant closed the door before saying, "Madeline Harper."

"Well, good morning, Miss Harper. This is Eddie with Home on the Range Properties. Is this a good time?"

Madeline almost laughed. Oh, sure, it was a fantastic time.

Couldn't be better. "It is," she replied, deciding not to indulge the need to have a nervous breakdown.

"I've got some good news this time around. Your rental house is finally ready. Is there a good time for me to drop off the keys for you?"

It was about time. Apparently Sunnybell didn't believe in anything as practical as apartments, so she'd been forced to wait until a suitable rental house became free. The timing, however, couldn't have been better. It was her excuse to escape and regroup, and she grasped it like the lifeline it was. "You know what? Stay where you are. I'll come to you."

Mr. Westerfield, her job, and the busybodies of this town would just have to wait. She had a house to move into. She'd spend the weekend hiding out there and then maybe, if she was very, very lucky, this whole thing would blow over by Monday.

And maybe it would rain diamonds, too.

Life on the rodeo circuit wasn't glamorous, but it was a hell of a lot more exciting than Tanner's new life, that was for damn sure. Trudging through the aisles of Harrison Hardware and Supply Company on a Saturday morning with a neatly ordered list written out by his grandmother and double-checked by Grandpa Jack was not his idea of a good time.

But he had made a promise to them. If they wanted him to pick up a half dozen new feed buckets and a "cushier"-handled garden trowel, then by God, he'd do it. Honestly, he'd do just about anything for either one of them.

As he turned the corner into the garden tool aisle, he came to an abrupt halt, his eyes widening. Before him stood Miss New York herself, her blond hair tucked in a short ponytail and her long legs on display beneath a pair of green-and-white polka-dot shorts.

The mere sight of her made his pulse kick up. The night they'd spent together had seemed too good to be true. A slow smile turned up the corners of his mouth. He didn't know why she was still in town, but he had never been one to look a gift horse in the mouth.

Sauntering over to where she stood staring at rakes as if they were a foreign language, he said, "Afternoon. Shopping for souvenirs, are we?"

She sucked in a surprised breath and whirled to face him. Her cheeks turned a pretty shade of pink as she locked eyes with him. "Souvenirs?"

He grinned and picked up one of the rakes, turning it in his hands a few times. "Well, I don't imagine those New York City stores sell many gardening tools."

Since her car hadn't been in the motel parking lot that morning, he'd thought she was already on her way back. He hadn't expected to run into her again, but, seeing her now in her cute little shorts and her off-the-shoulder sweatshirt made him glad he'd been wrong.

Narrowing her eyes, she reached out and chose a different rake. "You can get anything in New York," she said, her voice cool and her words clipped. "And no, this is not a souvenir.

This is a tool to improve the atrocious state of my lawn, thank you very much."

Her *lawn*? He took a cautious step back. "Do you commute to the city then?"

She gave a half laugh, half snort. "Kind of hard to commute to the city from here, cowboy."

He stiffened. What in the world was she talking about? Wariness straightened his spine as he set the handle of the rake against the concrete floor. "Here meaning…?"

She gestured vaguely around them. "Here," she said, as though the meaning should be obvious. Her hand settled at her hip as she turned accusing eyes on him. "Speaking of which, why the hell didn't you tell me you were some sort of local celebrity?"

"Whoa," he said, holding up his free hand, palm out. "Hold on there. I don't remember you being real keen to exchange biographies and resumes out on the dance floor, or between the sheets, for that matter. Hell, I still don't even know your name."

She drew a deep breath, trying to rein in her temper. Spreading her lips into a forced smile, she stalked forward and thrust out her hand. "Hello, Tanner Callen, local rodeo star and apparent town golden child. I'm Madeline Harper. Your new neighbor."

# Chapter 5

THE STRING OF curses that ran through Tanner's mind would have earned him a pair of boxed ears from his grandmother. His hot out-of-towner hookup was his *neighbor*?

"You're moving here?" he asked dumbly, staring back at her in shock.

"Correction: I've moved here. Past tense." She looked no more pleased about it than he was.

How the hell could this be? She drove a car with New York plates. She'd been staying at the local motel. Hell, she talked like a damn Kennedy. He ran a hand through his hair, feeling as though he'd been set up. "You're complaining that I didn't tell you I was a former rodeo competitor, when you didn't see fit to tell me that you were fixing to put down stakes here?"

She bit her lip and tightened her grip on the wooden handle. "It didn't come up," she said, half defensive, half sheepish.

"Yeah, well, neither did my former profession." He jammed the rake back into the display. "Perhaps because it's 'past tense' as well. Your moving to Sunnybell seems much more relevant."

"You're right, it is. You know why?" She raised both eyebrows, daring him to answer. He knew better than to take the bait, and waited silently for her to continue, which she did almost immediately. "Because I don't want all my new co-workers making a habit of demanding details of my private life so they can get all the juicy details about what it's like to go to bed with *Callen the Stallion*."

Tanner nearly choked on thin air. There was a term he hadn't heard in years. His idiot friend Mack had thought it was hilarious to tease him with it back when they were on the circuit together, but the damn name had followed him back home somehow. He'd have to remember to thank his friend.

"You may be new here," he said, pointing at her before jabbing his finger at his own chest, "but I've spent my whole adult life avoiding being gossiped about. If I'd have known you were here to stay, I'd never have said two words to you."

She frowned. "What a lovely sentiment. Unfortunately, neither one of us can go back in time and un-ring that bell, so I suggest we just pretend that night never happened."

Tanner straightened, the comment hitting him all wrong. "Beg your pardon?"

He wasn't any happier about the situation than she was, but damned if he was going to pretend that they hadn't just about singed the sheets with the sparks flying between them. She was acting like nothing had happened, but he remembered every minute they'd spent pressed against each other.

"It was a mistake," she said, shaking her head. "A stupid

decision that I wish I could undo. Since that option's off the table, the next best thing is to forget we ever set eyes on each other in the first place."

He may have been poised to hightail it out of there like a deer in a hunter's sights not two minutes ago, but now? He planted his feet more firmly. His pride wasn't about to let her get away with pretending that their time together hadn't been about as charged as a lightning rod in a thunderstorm. He wouldn't have allowed things to happen as they had if he'd known she was here to stay, but he damn sure wasn't about to deny it now. And he could be right stubborn when he put his mind to something.

"I'm not sure that's possible, seeing how we're to be neighbors. And you know what? I was raised to be nothing if not neighborly," he drawled, sending her a lazy half smile. Stepping toward her, he grabbed the rake in her hands and tugged.

Taken off guard, she stumbled forward, stopping only inches from him.

He continued, his voice low and seductive. "So, neighbor, how 'bout I lend you a hand. Show you how this here rake works?"

The familiar sizzle of chemistry zinged between them, surprising him with its intensity. Her lips parted as her chest rose and fell with her suddenly fast breathing. In that moment, he remembered every kiss, every gasp, every satisfied sigh she'd breathed that night.

*Damn.* He should have walked away when he had the chance. Because God help him, it was too late now.

In her defense, she *really* hated yard work.

Nibbling her bottom lip, Madeline stood in the small wood-paneled kitchen of her rental house, watching the half-naked man raking her yard with a vengeance. No, there was no defense. He'd pulled her close, with challenge burning in those Tiffany-blue eyes, and she'd folded like a cheap card table.

Holding her head high, she'd said, "If you wish to dabble in unpaid landscaping, be my guest." To which he'd grinned, grabbed her rake, and headed for the checkout.

And everything had been fine until the shirt had come off.

Why did it have to be so hot here, anyway? It was November, for Pete's sake. Sweater weather. The time for boots and cute coats and pumpkin spice lattes. Leave it to Texas to have a November day hot enough to make her sweat. Well, technically it was making *him* sweat, causing the shirt removal, which in turn caused her to sweat, but still, it was the weather's fault.

She sighed. Fine—it was her fault, too. She should have been smart enough to tell him where he could put that rake and his knowing smiles, but, well, back to those eyes and her hatred of yard work. Vicious cycle, really.

He paused to swipe his arm over his forehead, and she did what any good friend would do: she snapped a quick picture and texted it to Aisha and Brianna. The immediate, drooling responses she received from both of them made her laugh out loud.

Setting her phone down, she leaned against the window frame and watched as he bent over and gathered up an armful of yard debris and stuffed it into a bag beside him. It was impossible not to notice the way the sunshine gleamed off his skin, outlining each and every contour.

When Tanner straightened, he glanced over to catch her watching him. She jerked to attention and backed away from the window, spilling half her drink down her shirt in the process. She cursed and grabbed the dish towel from the counter, mopping up as much as she could from her shirt before turning her attention to the floor.

This was not like her. She did not go around staring at shirtless men and tripping over her feet like some sort of clumsy schoolgirl. She was a smart, savvy businesswoman who had taken a half decade's worth of ballet in her formative years so that she'd learn to move gracefully. She absolutely refused to be undone by a man who she knew was only working in her yard to prove some sort of point.

And yes, she knew exactly how convoluted that sounded.

The hollow knock of knuckles on the aluminum storm door rang out, and she looked up to see Tanner standing on the other side. His loose grin and bright eyes made it seem like he knew every thought she'd had about him over the last hour, which immediately put her on the defensive.

Straightening, she walked to the door, crossing her arms over the damp spot on her shirt. "Need something?"

He set a hand to his flat stomach and lifted an eyebrow. "Awful thirsty."

It was like he knew his abs were her own personal kryptonite. She forced her gaze not to stray from his eyes. "You're in luck," she said brightly. "I've arranged for an endless supply of cool, crystal-clear water just for you." She nodded toward the hose.

He didn't move, and actually seemed a little amused. "A man could use a cold beer on a day like this."

"I agree completely. Why don't you grab yourself one on the way home. You've definitely earned it." She gave him her most impersonal smile.

"Not exactly what I had in mind," he drawled, pushing his hat up an inch with his thumb. A lock of dark, damp hair fell across his forehead.

"I know, but life is disappointing sometimes. Thanks for the help, though. I do appreciate it." Nodding once, she closed the door.

There. See? She could resist him. And she could *definitely* resist the effect his presence in her life had on her work persona. Whenever she felt herself softening, she needed to remember the looks on her coworkers' faces yesterday. She hoped she'd never feel that sort of mortification again, let alone at her workplace.

She'd allowed herself to be drawn in by his challenging gaze, but hoped disappointing him now would put an end to whatever might happen between them.

Two hours later, she'd scrubbed every last greasy morsel

from the kitchen until it was finally to the point where the thought of walking barefoot on the 1970s linoleum didn't gross her out. Her back ached, her fingers were tired, and the smell of bleach seemed to have taken up permanent residence in her nose. Tossing her yellow gloves in the sink, she stood and stretched. One room would have to be enough for the day.

Out of the corner of her eye, movement snagged her attention. She started to walk over to the window but came to an abrupt halt, her mouth dropping open.

*What in the world?* Her yard was immaculate. All the weeds, scrabbly brush, and debris were completely gone. It was neat as a pin, as though someone hadn't completely neglected it for the past five years or so. But…she'd thought it would have taken days to tackle that mess. Moreover, she'd assumed Tanner had packed up and left after she'd shut the door on him.

But he'd stayed. He'd finished it. Why?

Madeline saw the movement again and glanced to the right. Her stomach flipped. There stood her yard-hero cowboy, sweat-stained, exhausted-looking, and gulping water from the hose as though he hadn't had a drink in days. She looked back to the spotless yard. She couldn't believe he'd worked so hard for her, especially after the frosty way she'd treated him.

She groaned, her nose wrinkled in distaste. *Crap.* She had no choice but to go make nice with the man now. The very thought made her blood pump faster. Taking a deep, bracing breath, she opened the door and headed outside.

## Chapter 6

THE TELLTALE CREAK of the storm door opening might well have been the sweetest sound Tanner had ever heard. It was the sound of victory, after all.

Wiping the moisture from his chin with the back of his hand, he straightened and turned toward the door, resisting the urge to grin. There Miss Madeline Harper stood, her lips pursed and her arms crossed over her chest. Her ponytail was no longer neat, with wispy blond hairs haphazardly framing her face. A few smudges decorated her forehead, like she'd been swiping at her hair with dirty fingers, though her hands looked perfectly clean from here.

He liked her this way. Made her look less standoffish, even with the half scowl still wrinkling her brow.

Anyone with a lick of sense would have packed up and left after she'd shut the door, both literally and figuratively. But Tanner had two reasons to stay: Grandpa Jack had taught him that a man finished what he started, and there was a sort of perverse satisfaction that came from staying put when she expected him to turn tail and flee.

When she didn't speak right away, he pulled his shirt out of his back pocket and put it on, giving her time to say whatever was stuck on the end of her tongue.

After a moment, she cleared her throat and pressed her lips into an unconvincing smile. "You really didn't have to do all this work today."

He did smile then. "Is that a thank-you? I don't quite speak Yankee, so it's hard to tell."

He couldn't tell if she was biting back a grimace or a grin. Blowing out a breath, she said, "Thank you. Though I never asked for your help, it was very nice of you to offer it."

He leaned forward and rested his arms on the black wrought iron railing of the steps. "'Round here, people don't have to ask for help. If we see a need, we fill it."

"And what if they don't want it?" Challenge gleamed behind those pretty gold-flecked brown eyes of hers. He'd have never guessed she was this stubborn after their first night together.

"Not wanting it and not asking for it are two different things. The way I see it, if you didn't want me here, you wouldn't have led the way." He shrugged, looking up at her. "Or do you wish I'd have left you to it?"

She dropped her arms to her hips. "I could have done it. I *would* have done it."

"No one said you couldn't. And that wasn't the question."

He pushed back from the railing and walked around to stand on the small concrete landing. "Would you rather I didn't come today?"

He lifted an eyebrow, daring her to say no. Daring her to lie and say she wished he'd stayed away. Because it would be a lie; he could see it in her eyes.

He watched her throat work as she swallowed and shook her head. "No, I wouldn't. I appreciate your hard work." The words sounded slightly wooden, but he knew she was the kind of girl who didn't back down easy, so he considered it a win.

Smiling, he grabbed his hat from the end of the railing and put it on for the sole purpose of tipping it. "Glad to be of service."

"I'm curious, though," she said, walking down a step. "If you don't want to be gossiped about, why risk coming here?"

Grandpa Jack's voice echoed in the back of his mind. *Pride goes before a fall.* He shouldn't have come here today, especially after what she had said about her coworkers, but his pride had gotten in the way. Ironically, pride kept him from saying as much to Madeline. Instead, he shrugged and pointed to the only neighbors visible from her property. "Old Mr. Winters is visiting his sister this month, and Mrs. White is as blind as a deaf bat. I'd say we're safe for now."

"Oh. Well, in that case, I can offer you dinner. By way of thanks, of course."

It was a tentative invitation, spoken hesitantly, but it was a definite in. He had her now. Letting his lips curl up just a bit, he shook his head. "I couldn't trouble you like that. I know you never asked me here in the first place."

Another step down. "No, really. You earned it, as hard as you worked."

A soft breeze ruffled the hair at her temples, and she brushed it back with impatient fingers. He knew she'd worked the afternoon away, same as him. He'd caught glimpses of her in the kitchen windows, moving this way and that.

"You worked hard, too. No need to work more on my account."

She grinned then, the first genuine smile he'd seen since the night they'd met. He felt it all the way to the pit of his belly. "Trust me, there's no work involved. Frozen pizza and soda, dinner of champions."

His smile was genuine as well. "Sounds good to me. Are you sure you want me to stay?"

Pulling her top lip between her teeth for a moment, she gave him a look that said that she knew exactly what he was doing. He wanted her to admit that she wanted him to stay. Yes, he was teasing her into it, but that was what made it fun.

He could tell she was reluctantly amused, even as she rolled her eyes. "Yes."

"Yes, what?"

Wrinkling her nose, she set her hands to her hips and said, "I want you to stay. It's the least I can do."

*Success!* Dipping his head magnanimously in acceptance of her invitation, he grinned. "Well, if you insist."

\*    \*    \*

As Madeline led him into the small, sparkling clean kitchen, she kept shaking her head, amazed that she'd extended the invitation. She'd meant it, though, when she'd said it was the least she could do. He'd done her a huge favor, and she wasn't about to let her lingering embarrassment get in the way of fairness or good manners.

Still, her stomach was doing that weird flipping thing, which was not a good sign. She tried to will the feeling away. This was just to thank him for his hard work, nothing more and nothing less. Turning to face him, she gestured toward the newly scoured stainless steel sink. "Feel free to wash your hands, if you like."

He nodded and reached for the soap. As he lathered up, she flipped on the decades-old stove and retrieved one of the frozen pizzas she'd bought last night at a natural foods grocery store in San Antonio. She'd driven over an hour out of her way just to be sure she wouldn't run into anyone she knew. Too bad she hadn't done the same for her hardware store trip. If she had, she wouldn't be standing in the kitchen with Tanner, trying not to notice how much space he commanded in the small room.

As she set the box on the counter, she asked, "What do you want to drink? I have water, milk, and diet Coke."

He shook off his hands, grabbed a paper towel, and turned to face her. "Good to know you weren't just being cruel and unusual about the beer earlier," he said with a wink as he dried his hands. "Ice water's fine, thanks."

"I've got tap water, hose water, or warm bottled water that I forgot to get out of my trunk. It never occurred to me that I'd have to add ice trays to my shopping list when I was picking up essentials yesterday." She'd never even seen a fridge without an icemaker before. Then again, she'd never seen a kitchen that was 99 percent wood or wood veneer, either.

"Such a sheltered life," he deadpanned, shaking his head. That trademark smile tilted his lips as he tipped his chin toward the sink. "Tap water's fine. When you've lived a life like mine, you learn to take what you can get."

He turned to toss the towel in the garbage and caught sight of the pizza box. "Hold up. I thought you said you had frozen pizza. What the heck is that?" He picked it up, making a face as if it were a box of liverwurst.

"Goat cheese and spinach flatbread. It's delicious," she said, grabbing the box back from him. "And didn't you just say that you take what you can get?"

"A man has his limits. Let me see that. I want to know if it's made with twigs and granola, too."

He leaned forward to grab it from her, and she quickly swung it behind her back, laughing. "It's good, I promise. You need to try new things."

In two steps he trapped her against the cabinet, his hands on either side of her. Her heart raced at his nearness, and she stilled. Mirth lit his eyes, but so did something else. Something she didn't want to name, but that her body seemed to recognize.

He leaned closer, bringing his face only inches from hers. The scent of sunshine, salty sweat, and *him* filled her nostrils. "I love new things. But that doesn't mean I'm going to eat grass-flavored cardboard." His voice had gone slightly husky, as though roughened with fine-grit sandpaper, even as it was light with teasing.

Swallowing, she ducked out from under his arm and stepped far enough away that she could breathe again. "Well, you're out of luck then, because that's all I have in the house." Butterflies whirled in her belly, and she took a long, slow breath to try to get herself back under control.

He turned and leaned back against the counter, his eyes sparking once again with challenge. As he watched her for a moment, the corners of his mouth still tilted up, she stifled the urge to blush under the weight of his gaze. At last he nodded, as though coming to a decision. "Get your purse."

"What?" She blinked back at him, surprised by the command.

"Get your purse," he said again, this time more persuasively. "I'm going to show you what real food tastes like."

# Chapter 7

TANNER WAS PROBABLY asking for trouble.

Okay, he was definitely asking for trouble, but right then, he didn't much care. Something about her seemed to shake all the good sense right out of his head. She brought out the impulsiveness that he thought he'd left behind with his early rodeo days, and for some reason he didn't want to fight it.

Madeline, on the other hand, seemed determined to fight it for him. He could practically see her earlier resolve cool the warmth that was there when she'd laughed a second ago.

Back to square one, he thought grimly.

Stepping back, she shook her head decisively. "I'm not going to get my purse, thank you, and I'm definitely not going out to eat with you."

She said it as though he'd suggested they skinny-dip in the town's memorial fountain at high noon. It hit him all wrong, especially after the playfulness they'd just had. He crossed his arms and scowled at her. "And why is that?"

"Tanner, I thought I made this clear. I don't want to be

seen with you. If you hadn't wooed me with promises of free yard work, you wouldn't even be here now." She blew out a short breath, stirring the loose hairs around her face. "It was a stupid move on my part, and I'm not going to make it worse by going out with you."

He gritted his teeth together. Well, if that didn't beat all. Here he was, offering to feed the woman after slaving away in her yard all day, and suddenly she was acting like she'd as soon dine with a raccoon than eat with him.

What had happened to the fun, sexy stranger he'd spent the night with? The chemistry was still there; that was for damn sure. He'd seen the widening of her eyes and the quick rise of her chest when he'd trapped her against the cabinet. He'd *felt* the pull between them, clear as day.

But something else was in her eyes now as she looked at him with her chin lifted and her shoulders ramrod straight. If he didn't know any better, he'd say it looked a lot like regret. Why? For having him over now, or for tangling with him in the first place?

Hell, she probably thought she was too good for someone like him, what with her fancy car, designer clothes, and Ivy League education. She saw little more than a man in a sweat-stained tee shirt and old, worn-out jeans and boots—his favorites, of course—sullying her kitchen while his old Chevy hunkered in her driveway.

He shook his head, wondering why he had bothered when she'd so clearly wanted to avoid him this morning. Pride and the love of a good challenge were a dangerous mix of personality traits.

"Thank you for the clarification," he said tersely. "My apologies for imposing myself on you. You can rest assured I won't do it again."

With a curt tip of his hat—manners were manners—he turned on his heel and stalked outside, letting the screen door slam behind him. He paused long enough to gather up the last two bags of lawn debris before making his way around the house to his truck. He tossed the bags in the back with more force than necessary before slamming the tailgate shut with a satisfying thud.

He wasn't used to rejection. Women liked him, and he liked them. But this was more than just a woman turning down his attentions. Madeline was something different. There was a sizzle between them that had robbed him of his better judgment. Spending time with her gave him the same sort of risky thrill riding a bucking bronco always had—a feeling he'd missed like hell since leaving the circuit.

Even so, he'd be damned if he'd butt in where he wasn't wanted.

He walked around to the driver's side door and pulled it open, ignoring the familiar squeak of the old hinges. The truck had belonged to his father, and he loved everything about the old rust bucket. And really, after all his years on the circuit, Tanner could relate to the truck's wheezes and groans.

He put one foot up on the running board when the sound

of his name brought him up short. Glancing up, he saw Madeline jogging around the side of the house, her ponytail swinging. He narrowed his eyes but stayed where he was. Now what? He rested his elbows on the ledge of the open window and waited for her to reach him.

She stopped just on the other side of the car door. "That came out all wrong," she said, a little out of breath. She paused to draw in a steadying lungful of air before setting her golden gaze squarely on him. "It's not you. I'm just…overly protective of my reputation here."

"Ah, the old 'it's not you, it's me' line," he drawled, one eyebrow lifted.

"I'm serious," she said, stepping closer in her earnestness and setting one hand on the door ledge beside his elbow. "I like you, and I'm sorry if I came across as ungrateful or rude, but it was a shock having my coworkers dissect my personal life. This merger is the biggest thing ever to happen to my career, and I won't derail it by losing my colleagues' respect."

He wanted to make another smart remark but stifled it. It was big of her to come after him like this, and he really couldn't fault her for not wanting to be gossiped about. He'd spent his entire adult life doing the same. "People won't respect you less for making friends, Madeline."

She gave a short laugh. "Is that what we're doing?" she said wryly. "I want the people here to take me seriously, and I don't think that'll happen if I get involved with the local heartthrob. I'm not giving all the local Tanner fans further reason to hate me, thank you very much."

*"Heartthrob?"* he said, letting out a crack of laughter. "I suppose I should be flattered."

Rolling her eyes, she said, "As if you didn't know what the women in this town think of you." Her lips tugged into a small grin.

"I'm more interested in what you think of me," he replied lightly, only half teasing. "But all that aside, you, Miss Harper, jumped to conclusions."

Her eyebrows tilted up. "About what?"

"You assumed that I was ignoring the fact that you wanted to stay beneath the gossip radar. I understand that you don't want to draw attention to us, and I respect that."

"But you asked me to go out to eat with you. How else was I to interpret that? There are like two restaurants in this whole town. It'd be impossible not to be seen."

"Now, see, that's where you're wrong," he said, letting the words percolate in a bit of mystery. He climbed into the truck and pulled the door closed. Leaning his head through the open window, he gave her a challenging grin and nodded toward the passenger side. "Get in."

She looked unconvinced, but he could see he'd piqued her interest. "I don't have my purse. Or my phone, for that matter. And where do you want to go?"

He turned the key and the old truck roared to life. "You don't need either where we're going. Just trust me." For some reason, it was important to him that she have a little faith in him. If she didn't, then he'd know for sure that she didn't believe he was a man of his word.

For a few seconds, she stood rooted in place. He held his breath, wanting her to agree, but wanting more for her to *want* to agree. Finally, she shot him a wide, adventurous smile that he felt all the way to the pit of his stomach. She'd taken the bait.

Coming around to the passenger side, she pulled open the door and climbed in. "Alright, cowboy. I'll trust you. Don't make me regret it."

Triumph and excitement warmed his blood as he sent her a crooked smile and thumbed the brim of his hat. "Yes ma'am. You have my word."

# Chapter 8

IT WAS THE lawn bag pickup that had done her in.

Madeline had stood firm in her determination to cut ties with Tanner all the way up until the moment he had stopped to gather the rest of the trash bags and carry them from her yard. Who does that after being told, in no uncertain terms, to hit the road?

It had made her feel like a complete jerk. Worse, an ungrateful jerk. He had worked so hard all day long, and even after being kicked to the curb, he'd still followed through with his commitment to help her. Her conscience wouldn't let her leave things as they were.

An apology was one thing, but jumping into his truck on a whim, sans purse and phone, was another thing altogether. She wasn't the impulsive or adventurous type—slow and steady won the race, and all that—but here she was, bumping along a dirt road in a truck that was probably older than her preschool diploma, trusting a guy she'd known less than a week with not only her reputation but her well-being.

She pressed her lips together, keeping her eyes on the rugged landscape ahead of them. Even though she didn't regret it—yet—she had to wonder what had possessed her to do such a thing. His honest eyes? That crooked grin? Perhaps she'd just gone ab-blind after catching glimpses of his impressive bare torso all day, and hadn't quite regained her senses.

Whatever it was, she couldn't even bring herself to be chagrined by it. She really did trust him, no matter how illogical that sounded. For all his flirting and sparring with her, he was a good guy. He had a truck bed full of lawn bags and an entire town's devotion to prove it.

As they crested a small rise, she caught sight of a quaint log cabin up ahead. A pair of rocking chairs sat on the wide covered porch, and flowers spilled from a half barrel at the foot of the stairs. Red-and-white gingham curtains fluttered in the open windows while a few metal whirligigs spun away in the garden. The sweet whimsy of the place made her smile.

Farther past the drive sat a picturesque red barn, with a circular paddock on one side. Wide-open pastureland extended as far as she could see, with a smattering of long-horned cattle grazing the scrubby grasses. The whole place looked timeless, as though it could have been built anywhere from five to a hundred years ago.

Tanner slowed and turned into the driveway, and she couldn't help but glance at him in surprise. He caught the look and grinned back. "Welcome to Casa Callen."

"You live here?" She didn't mean to sound incredulous, but the place was so homey. She pictured a sweet old grandmother baking pies in the kitchen while her suspender-wearing husband tended the garden.

"I live here," he confirmed as he put the truck into park and killed the engine. Even with the windows down, the quiet was profound. It had been at least five minutes since they'd passed another house.

A wry grin came to her lips as she looked around at the wilderness surrounding them. "No wonder you weren't concerned for my reputation."

His chuckle was rough and warm. "Well, the cows can be damn nosy sometimes, but other than that, you could run buck naked for miles and no one would be the wiser." Tossing her a wicked grin, he added, "So feel free."

"I'm good, thanks," she said with a lighthearted roll of her eyes. Normally she'd hate being so far from civilization, but there was something thrilling about being out here with Tanner, completely alone. She swallowed, keeping her thoughts in check. She was here for dinner, nothing more. No matter how sexy the man was, she couldn't afford to get involved with him. Eventually her fluttering stomach would remember that.

She hoped.

"Come on, I'll give you the grand tour." He unbuckled his seat belt and hopped out of the truck. By the time she undid her own seat belt, he was at her side, pulling the door open for her. "Careful now," he said, holding out his hands. "The running board on this side is a little rusted."

Swallowing, she set her hands on his shoulders and allowed him to lift her. He set her down just a little too close to him, and for a moment she feared—hoped?—that he would steal a kiss. Memories of his hands against her bare skin in her motel room made her breath catch, and she glanced away, afraid he would see the flash of attraction in her eyes.

Thankfully, he was a perfect gentleman, stepping back and sweeping his hand toward the house. "After you."

They made their way down the flagstone path before climbing the four stairs to the front door. She expected him to pull out his keys to unlock the door, but he simply turned the knob and swung it open. She shook her head. Even a thousand miles from anyone, she would probably still lock her doors. It was as ingrained in her as brushing her teeth or fastening her seat belt.

"Lived here long?" she asked as she followed him inside. It was small by Texas standards, but cozy, with simple, comfortable-looking furniture and plain white walls. The only decorations were several carved wood horses and a few surprisingly lovely oil landscape paintings.

"It was my parents' place when they married. Mom sold it to me when she moved to Austin a few years back."

"Oh, so you grew up here," she said, looking around with renewed interest. It was easy to imagine little booted feet scuffing the wide-plank pine floors while running laps around the connected kitchen, dining, and living rooms.

His mouth tightened a bit as he shook his head. "Not really. It's a long story," he added with a dismissive wave of his hand. "Kitchen's this way."

Her curiosity flared, but she let it lie as she followed him into the room at the back of the house, which was surprisingly modern. The cabinets were still made of the same warm wood as the rest of the house, but gleaming stainless steel appliances and glittering granite countertops gave it an extra element of style that she had to admire.

"I'm hungry enough to eat a horse. You?" he asked, opening the fridge and pulling out a pair of steaks big enough to each fill a dinner plate on their own. As he turned to rummage in the vegetable drawer, she bit the inside of her lip and grimaced.

"I am, but I should have said earlier that I'm a vegetarian." She waited for the inevitable mocking comment or look of contempt. He probably had a beef-jerky pacifier as a baby, judging by his surroundings.

But to her surprise, he simply returned one of the steaks to the fridge and grabbed an armload of mushrooms, peppers, and zucchini instead. He paused when he caught a glimpse of her shocked expression and shrugged, a hint of a grin curling the corners of his mouth. "A person's preferences are his or her own, Madeline. If you're not offended by my choices, I'm not offended by yours."

She blinked. Well. How very modern of him. It seemed like people always had something to say about her choice not to eat meat. His response was unexpected, and nice. Really nice.

"Besides," he added, with an appreciative sweep of her figure, "whatever you are doing is obviously working for you."

His devilish wink made her laugh, even as it sent a rush of butterflies through her belly. She bit back a grin and went to wash her hands, trying to shrug off the effect he had on her. "Where's the cutting board?" she asked lightly, as though he hadn't just made her blush like a schoolgirl.

"I'll take care of this," he said, coming up behind her close enough to make her shiver, without actually touching her. He reached over her shoulder and retrieved a wineglass from the cabinet by her shoulder. "You go have a seat and enjoy a little wine."

She opened her mouth to argue, then thought better of it. After two days of cleaning and unpacking, she wasn't going to turn down the suggestion. Drying her hands on a dish towel, she turned to face him and offered a wry smile. "Don't say it unless you mean it."

"Darlin'," he said, leaning forward just enough to make her heart pound, "when it comes to me, you can rest assured that I always tell the truth, I never turn down a challenge, and I *always* say what I mean."

With that, he held up the glass, his blue eyes sparkling. There was no missing the warm promise in both his gaze and his deep voice, a promise that had nothing to do with wine or dinner.

Lifting her chin, she plucked the glass from his fingers and smiled. "In that case, will you be serving red or white?"

He chuckled and shook his head. "Haven't you figured it out yet? 'Round here, it's always ladies' choice."

By the time dinner was ready, Madeline was thoroughly relaxed and happy. She'd never had a man cook for her before. Where she lived, it was a choice between going out or ordering in, as her tiny kitchen was hardly worth hassling with.

Watching Tanner cook was actually an enjoyable experience. She liked watching his easy, capable movements as he sliced the veggies, prepared the kabobs and salads, and stood guard at the grill. He wasn't putting on a show; clearly he enjoyed cooking. She'd even missed him when he'd dashed inside for the world's fastest shower, reappearing less than five minutes later with his hair damp and tousled in order to flip the steak.

As they sat down to eat at the oval-shaped table on the back deck, the two of them on the same side in order to face the view, she gave an appreciative nod at the quality of the meal. "I wouldn't think there'd be much time to learn to cook on the road as a rodeo star," she said before taking her first bite of the baked potato. She almost groaned in pleasure at its buttery, cheesy goodness. It was worth every last carb, as far as she was concerned.

He shook his head as he washed down a mouthful of salad with a swig of his beer. "There wasn't. But my grandmother made sure I knew how to cook a proper spread before I could even drive. I'm grateful to her, since eating out gets old in a hurry. And it's such a hassle to go out to eat when I'm home, living as far away as I do. Lucky for me, I enjoy cooking."

She savored a slice of perfectly tender grilled zucchini before murmuring, "Lucky for me, too."

That made him smile, which in turn made her do the same. The soft evening breeze tugged at his rapidly drying hair while the setting sun made his eyes sparkle. He looked like a model fresh off a shoot for a Country Living magazine. Seriously, the man was ridiculously handsome.

And it was almost too intimate, smiling together on his back deck, nothing but cattle and wilderness around for miles. Suddenly self-conscious, she looked down at her plate. She fumbled around for a new topic of conversation as she chased a cherry tomato around her plate. "So do you work here now? I mean, now that you are a *former* rodeo star, if office gossip is to be believed."

She looked up just in time to catch his boyish, tilted grin. "Who you callin' 'former'? Being a rodeo champion is like being a triathlete: once you've done the deed, the title is yours for keeps."

He was clearly teasing, and she found herself smiling back at him all over again. "I stand corrected. So is the retired champion resting on his laurels now?"

"Naw. I spend most days helping out on my grandfather's ranch. You can see the property line, just over that ridge." He tipped his chin toward the sunset, where a narrow footpath disappeared over a rise. She hadn't noticed the barbed wire fence cutting across the land there before.

She frowned. "You walk to work?" It seemed like everyone drove everywhere in Texas, including to the mailbox.

He shook his head, amused. "I ride to work. I'd spend half the day commuting if I had to walk."

"Like, on a *horse?*" Did people actually do that? Outside of a movie set, that was. It seemed to her like a fast way to break a neck.

That made him laugh out loud. "Yes, on a horse. The cattle would have me on my ass if I ever tried to ride them. That's the life I've left behind," he added with a good-natured wink.

"Well, how should I know?" she asked, wrinkling her nose at his teasing. "It's not like this is the Wild West. People use cars and bikes now. You do know we've put a man on the moon, yes?"

"Have we, now?" he asked, pretending to be impressed with the idea. "What'll they think of next?"

It was her turn to laugh. He definitely didn't take himself too seriously. "Skyscrapers. Taxis. Chinese food delivery."

"You don't say," he drawled before taking a bite of steak. "Tell me more."

She sat back in her chair and sighed. She missed the city so much. Just thinking about the place she considered to be home made her heart ache. "Have you ever been to New York?"

He shook his head.

"Now that is a travesty. It's especially gorgeous this time of year, with the trees still holding onto a little color before winter sets in. The sky is never bluer than it is in autumn, too. There's so much *life* there. So much noise and bustle. You're never alone when you're in the city."

He quirked an eyebrow. "Which is why I've never been. Y'all are packed in that city like sardines. Give me the wide-open spaces and solitude any day of the week."

His answer didn't surprise her, but it was still unfair. She leaned forward, wanting him to open his mind and listen. "You only think that because you've never given the city a chance. There's so much culture there. So many amazing restaurants and random, fun little stores. If you can't find something in New York, it doesn't exist."

"What about peace and quiet?"

She rolled her eyes. "I should have said, if you can't find it in New York, you don't need it."

"Yet you had to come all the way to Texas to find a date."

He laughed when she swatted at him. She shook her head even as she suppressed a grin. "Very funny. And this is *not* a date."

"'Course not," he said easily, his rough velvet voice nearly a caress.

She wondered if he really did think of this as a date, even

if he wouldn't call it that. It was so strange, sitting here with a man who knew her body as well as he did, trying to act as if she didn't find him as attractive as hell. She didn't *want* to. She'd only agreed to come with him out of guilt for her rude behavior toward him…hadn't she?

She swallowed, refusing to admit otherwise.

Leaning forward, he casually swiped a finger over her chin, causing her to pause mid-chew. "Potato," he said by way of explanation before settling back in his chair. "So if everything you need in the world is in New York City, why are you sitting on my deck in Sunnybell?"

She resisted the desire to shiver from his small touch. "Merely a means to an end." She took a quick, bracing drink of wine before expounding. "I'd been at the company for five years, slowly working my way up, when six weeks ago my immediate boss quit unexpectedly. We had already been working on the merger for months, and the CEO of the entire company called me into his gorgeous corner office to ask if I could take over Marcus's job."

She shook her head, still marveling at the lucky break. "I've never jumped at something so fast in my life. One minute I'm running numbers and doing research, and the next I'm packing for a move to the middle of nowhere, Texas."

"You gave up the city you love and all your friends for your career?" He sounded genuinely taken aback. "Correct me if I'm wrong, but you miss home like a lost calf misses his mama's teat."

She straightened, feeling a little defensive. "I didn't give them up long-term. I'll only be here for a year, possibly two, before I'll be transferred back. Corporate only needs someone here through the transition and restructuring phases."

He nodded slowly, setting his fork down. "So what exactly do you do?"

"I'm Calvin Aviation Supply's youngest-ever acquisitions division manager. It's my job to keep things running smoothly during mergers."

He gave a low, appreciative whistle. "Sounds pretty highfalutin. No wonder you're so keen to command your coworkers' respect. I imagine there's a lot riding on your job performance, what with being the youngest and all."

That was an understatement.

Just talking about it made her shoulders tense up. She had so much to prove with this project. Normally, they never would have promoted her without a lengthy hiring process, but Marcus had left them in the lurch, and she was the person in the company who knew the project best.

She had to be on her game, since technically the job wouldn't be considered permanent until a three-month probation period was up. Legal was handling most of the details of the actual merger at this point, but it was up to her to see that the transition went smoothly.

Taking a deep breath, she lifted her chin and smiled. "Nothing I can't handle."

"I don't doubt it. So what does a normal day look like for an acquisitions division manager?"

She waved a hand. "Nothing terribly exciting. I oversee the blending of companies while making sure Calvin maximizes profits. Lots of paperwork and boring phone calls involved."

"So no flying around in fancy corporate jets, showing off the company's products?"

Shuddering, she shook her head. "God, no. I hate flying. I'll do it if I have to, but I'd rather drive any day of the week." It was why she'd bought her car before leaving New York. She'd much rather drive for hours than be crammed into a metal tube and launched into thin air without any control.

He looked momentarily incredulous before giving a small laugh. "You work for an aviation company and hate flying? Well, don't that beat all."

She shrugged. "It's a sensible career, given my schooling. I have no doubt I'll reach the top of the corporate ladder in time." It was a carefully planned goal that had been laid out since she was young. Do well in school, choose a prudent career with plenty of room for advancement, and eventually retire with a tidy nest egg.

Turning the conversation back to him, she said, "What about you? What's your new title?"

For some reason, the question amused him. He wolfed down another bite of his steak and grinned. "Stall mucker. Hay bale mover. Supply getter. Vendor negotiator. Hand manager. Basically, if it needs doing, I'm the man to do it."

She paused in scraping out the last of her potato from the skin to look askance at him. "That's a lot of responsibility. And this is your grandfather's ranch?"

The pride that shone in his blue gaze was almost defiant. "On paper. Grandpa Jack had a heart attack a few months back, so I'm doing what I can to take the weight from his shoulders. Old codger's been trying to lure me back from the rodeo for years. I just didn't realize how far he'd go to get me to quit." He winked as he made the joke, but there was real concern behind his lighthearted smile.

Something inside her chest squeezed. "You gave up your rodeo career for him?" She had thought of him as the sort of devil-may-care drifter type, doing whatever he wanted in life, but she clearly hadn't given him enough credit.

"Yes. And I'd give up a lot more for the man. I owe him my life."

She blinked in surprise at the vehemence of his words. "Oh."

She lifted her wineglass but didn't take a sip. Rolling the stem between her fingers, she considered the situation. It was hard to imagine the kind of devotion she could see in his eyes. She loved her parents, but they had their own lives. The idea of giving up all she had worked for in order to be at their beck and call was so foreign, she couldn't quite wrap her head around it. Moreover, she couldn't imagine them ever asking.

Curiosity tugged at her. She didn't want to pry, but…actually, that was a lie. She really, really did want to pry.

What had his grandfather done to inspire such dedication? How had he saved Tanner's life?

Attempting to sound nonchalant, she said, "Is this your mother's parents?"

He shook his head. "My father's." He concentrated on cutting another piece of steak. He didn't seem to want to talk about the subject, but she couldn't shake her curiosity.

"Ah. And what does your dad do?"

Tanner looked up then, and she knew before he said it what he was going to say. "He's dead. Died when I was nine."

Her heart sank low in her chest, and she reached out and put a hand over his. "I'm so sorry. I didn't know." His skin was warm against her fingers. He didn't pull away, and she let the touch linger.

"It was a long time ago."

For a whole ten seconds, she held her tongue. When she couldn't take the suspense, she asked, "What happened? He must have been very young."

"He was twenty-eight," he said, almost matter-of-factly. He set down his fork, crossed his arms, and looked her straight in the eye. "And he died of a broken neck."

Madeline's hand flew to her mouth. "That's horrible!" Her heart went out to the little boy who had lost his father so young, especially in such an awful way. "How did it happen?"

The breeze ruffled the hair at his temple, and he lifted a hand to brush it away. His beautiful eyes seemed to shutter as he gave a one-shouldered shrug. "Just a stupid accident," he said at last, shaking his head.

"A car accident?"

"Nope." He blew out a breath and sat forward. "He was riding his horse when the mare spooked. She threw him, he hit wrong, and unfortunately, that was that."

# Chapter 9

HE WISHED SHE had left well enough alone.

Tanner pressed his lips together as he watched Madeline's reaction to the news. It was always the same. The same widening of eyes, the same jaw drop, the same realization. By the time she hit that last part, he'd already steeled himself for the inevitable response.

Gaping at him as though he were ten cents short of a dollar, she said, "How on earth did you get back on a horse, let alone start a career where you're regularly *thrown* from them?"

Even though he expected the reaction, disappointment washed through him. Why did people always feel the need to throw judgment on him and his choices?

He pushed his plate away and seized his beer. "I chose to grab life by the horns. If I had walked away from riding horses, I'd have been giving up something I love. For all the wrong reasons."

It was plain to see she didn't understand his reasoning at all. "Yeah, but you don't just ride well-trained horses. You put yourself in harm's way by getting on animals that want nothing more than to throw you off."

"Well, the point is to *not* get thrown off," he said drily before taking a long pull of his beer. Did she really think he hadn't heard this argument a hundred times before?

She shook her head and set her wineglass on the table with a clipped clink. "I can't believe you can be so flippant about your well-being. If I were you, I wouldn't go anywhere near the back of a horse."

"And if your loved one was killed in a car accident, would you avoid driving in a car?"

She made a face. "That's not the same at all. Driving is a necessity in our society. Riding the back of a bucking bronco is not."

Scoffing, he said, "Maybe not for you. But I refuse to live life in fear. Nothing makes me feel more alive than taking a risk, so as far as I'm concerned, riding a 'bucking bronco' *is* a necessity in my life."

"That's insane," she said, coming to her feet. "You shouldn't have to risk your life in order to feel alive."

He stood as well and stalked to the railing. "How would you know? You live a life so dry that you could give it all up in a snap to follow a job you don't even care about."

"I care about my career," she said indignantly. "And yes, I'm willing to make sacrifices to get ahead in it. I plan to live a long and productive life. That's more than I can say for you."

"Oh, really? You're so bored with your own job you don't even want to talk about it. Where's the passion in that?"

Her brow lowered over her golden eyes as she sent him a sour look. "Oh, come on. Who really loves their job? It's a means to an end. What I want is corporate success, to be respected, and to retire with enough money to live well for the rest of my days."

Retirement? She didn't even look thirty yet. Tanner set his bottle on the railing and spread his arms. "Don't you want to live well *now?*"

She rolled her eyes. "Of course, but we have to plan for the future, too. We're adults, for God's sake. You can't go following your passion without a thought for the rest of your life."

He snorted. "You have the rest of your life to worry about the rest of your life. And anyway, what does it matter to you how I live my life? At least I'm *living* it, and not just existing until I'm old enough to draw retirement."

"Yeah, because you're too shortsighted to ever *see* retirement. You'll be lucky if you even see old age."

"Well, thank you for the vote of confidence, Miss Ray of Sunshine." His sarcasm was palpable, and he wasn't the least bit sorry for it. "I'd rather go to my grave smiling than die a well-preserved old geezer with a bushel of money and no one or nothing to spend it on."

"Miss Realist is more like it," she said stubbornly, crossing her arms over her chest and leaning back against the railing. "I'm sorry, but the truth is you're reckless and immature."

"Is that so?"

"Yes, it is," she said, her eyes flashing. "And it's that kind of attitude that will leave you stuck forever in this go-nowhere town with your rattling, decades-old truck and plot of land that's one turn of the color wheel away from looking like a Mars landscape!"

Madeline sucked in a sharp breath, horrified that the words had actually come out of her mouth. How could she have gotten so carried away? If she could have called the words back, she would have in a heartbeat, but it was too late.

Tanner's eyes cooled to an icy blue as he took a step back. "Darlin', you don't know nothing about happiness. All I need is a roof over my head, food in my belly, and the occasional good lay. The first two are taken care of, and you're welcome to oblige the third any time."

She pressed her lips together to keep from flinching. She'd just insulted everything he loved and stood for, and she couldn't even say why. It was none of her business how he lived his life. Perhaps his criticism of her life had hit closer to home than she cared to admit, but even that was no excuse.

Still, his cold dismissal hurt. God, there was nothing about them that was compatible—at least not outside of the bedroom. Agreeing to come here tonight had been incredibly stupid. What had she been thinking?

Swallowing, she lifted her chin and said evenly, "I think it'd be best if you took me home."

"You bet. Let me just get the keys to my rattling old truck

and we can be on our way." He stalked toward the house, slid open the door, and disappeared inside.

She closed her eyes and sighed. Part of her wanted to go after him and beg for forgiveness, to tell him that she'd been a jerk and she was sorry, but a bigger part of her knew it was for the best to just leave things as they were. It was clear she couldn't spend time with him as a friend. Until a few minutes ago, she'd spent the whole night trying to ignore the almost palpable attraction between them.

No, it was best to have a clean break. When it came to Tanner Callen, she just couldn't be trusted to keep her head about her.

When he returned, keys in hand, and stomped down the steps to the flagstone path, she silently followed. Thank God he'd only had the half a beer. If they'd had to wait for him to sober up, she might have decided to walk home, even if it took all night.

Holding her head as high as her guilty conscience would allow, she followed him. As she climbed into the old truck and slammed the door, she couldn't suppress another sigh.

Her year in Sunnybell couldn't be over fast enough.

# Chapter 10

"I KNOW JUST what you need."

Madeline's attention snapped back to the present, and she blinked over at her assistant. "I'm sorry?"

Laurie Beth rolled her eyes and grinned. "Boss lady, you've been a million miles away this week. How about you take a break and come to my book club tonight?"

As much as she wanted to deny it, Madeline *had* been distracted this week. She still felt rotten about what she'd said to Tanner, and how frosty their parting had been. The women at the office had invited her out a few times that week, but she'd used the unpacking excuse to sit at home and wallow in the misery of being stuck here. All she wanted was to get in the car and not stop until she saw New Jersey in the rearview mirror.

"Thanks, but I think I'll pass. I doubt I've read the book, anyhow." Actually, she probably had read the book. Reading was her one true escape, and she'd devoured countless books since moving here. Thank God for e-readers, since there wasn't a bookstore around for miles.

Just another thing this town didn't offer.

Laurie Beth flapped a hand. "That don't make no never-mind. We never stay on topic more than five minutes, any-how. We're really there for wine, Clarita's famous cupcakes, and good old-fashioned gossip."

"Tempting, but no thanks."

Sitting in the chair on the other side of Madeline's desk, Laurie Beth leveled a persuasive stare at her. "Now, Ms. Harper, I'm not one to pry, but I have it on good authority that you finished unpacking days ago. Mrs. White's daughter Sierra said there haven't been any more boxes in the trash since garbage pickup day on Tuesday."

Despite Madeline's scowl, her assistant pressed on. "You need to get out and enjoy your new town! You'll have fun, I promise. Oh, and Mr. Harvey over at the general store said you're partial to chardonnay. Since Ms. Letty never hosts a book club without bottles of the stuff, I know we'll have you covered."

Madeline let out a long breath. Would she ever get used to all the noses in her business here? She opened her mouth to turn down the offer again but found herself hesitating. She was a social person. All this solitude had long past worn thin. And it wouldn't be a bad idea to put names to faces around here. At least then she'd know who was gossiping about her.

Squaring her shoulders, she nodded. "Alright, fine. Text me the details and I'll see if I can make it."

A triumphant grin lit Laurie Beth's face. "Perfect! Why

don't I pick you up at a quarter to seven? Ms. Letty lives out in the boondocks, and I wouldn't want you to get lost trying to find it in the dark."

"How about I meet you here and follow you over? That way we can leave whenever we are ready." Though she'd agree to come, she wanted an escape plan in case the night didn't go well.

As it turned out, Laurie Beth hadn't been exaggerating. By the time they pulled up to the quaint ranch house that night, Madeline was so turned around she doubted she could have found her way there with a police escort. She'd have to have Laurie Beth write out the directions home before she left.

What was it with these people and their desire to live in the middle of nowhere?

Shaking her head, Madeline stepped out onto the gravel drive and looked around. Muted laughter filtered from within the gaily lit house, while the late dusk light hinted toward wide-open spaces all around them. She took a bracing breath. This would be her first purposefully social experience in this town. She sincerely hoped it went better than her interactions with Tanner.

She ducked back into the car to grab the bottle of wine she had brought—there could never be too much chardonnay at a party—before following Laurie Beth to the front door. Before they could knock, it was flung open by a short, well-padded older woman with bouffant white hair and bright-red glasses.

"Goodness gracious, I thought y'all would never get here. Come in, come in," she said, waving them both inside.

Laurie Beth gave the woman a quick hug before gesturing to Madeline. "Ms. Letty, this is my new boss, Ms. Madeline Harper. She's from New York City!"

The older woman smiled widely before wrapping her in a hug that left Madeline a little flustered. New Yorkers did *not* hug at first meeting.

"I knew who you were by process of elimination," she said as she'd pulled away. "I can't *wait* to hear all about New York. The book was a snooze this month—it read slower than molasses in January, I swear—so I'm in dire need of some entertainment. Come on, let me introduce you to everyone, then you and I can find us a quiet corner for some quality conversation."

Madeline allowed Ms. Letty to sweep her along to the living room, where a dozen women were busily chatting. She made the introductions, and Madeline did her best to keep up with all the names and faces.

The last woman she met, Ashley, looked vaguely familiar, and suddenly, Madeline remembered where they'd met. "Oh," she said, snapping her fingers, "I remember you. You were the accomplished mechanical bull rider at The Rebel Yell."

The brunette brightened. "I'll take that as a compliment. Good to see you again. I'm sorry we didn't get a chance to chat more that night but, well, you seemed a little preoccupied." Her wink was subtle and friendly, but Madeline felt a blush rise to her cheeks anyway.

"Yes, well, I'm glad we had a chance to meet again." She cleared her throat and looked to Ms. Letty. "Would you by chance have a glass for this wine?"

"Does a cat have climbing gear?" she replied saucily before slipping her arm around Madeline's and steering them to the kitchen. "We've already got a bottle or six open, so please help yourself."

Armed with wine in one hand and a red velvet cupcake in the other, Madeline sat in on the meeting, observing more than participating despite having read the book. They were actually a well-read group, referencing a dozen other books in their discussion. For the first time, she felt as though she had something in common with her new neighbors. It helped that they were all so friendly and welcoming.

She smiled. It was fascinating, listening to them chat and banter, gossip and confide. They were so easy with each other, it seemed they'd been friends for decades.

They probably had been.

Some of the more colorful Texan phrases made her laugh out loud, like when one of the women declared that the heroine was as dumb as a soup sandwich, and when Ashley complained that her Bundt cake turned out as dry as a bag of sawdust in July. The others rushed to assure her it was delicious, but she just waved off their compliments and dunked it in her wine.

It felt good to laugh with these women, even if Madeline did feel a little out of place. When Ms. Letty crooked a finger at her while the others were debating how satisfying the ending was, Madeline readily followed her into the dining room.

"I can't hear another word about that silly book," the older woman said as she settled into the chair at the head of the table and took a healthy swig of her wine. "That main character was as dumb as a bag of hammers. Truth be told, I'd rather read a romance any day of the week, but this was Betty Anne's month to choose, and we all humored her and her it-ain't-over-till-somebody-dies literary tastes."

Madeline bit back a laugh. She hadn't disliked the book, but the heroine's little brother had died at the end in what felt like an emotionally manipulative climax. "I see," she said diplomatically when she realized a response was expected.

"Now then, I would much rather hear all about where you're from."

Madeline smiled and took the seat next to her. "What would you like to know?"

"Oh, honey, it don't matter. I've just always wanted to go and never made it happen. My husband would sooner walk barefoot in a briar patch than take a trip to New York City. I've had to make do with *Law and Order* and *Sex and the City* for my NYC fix. Tell me *everything.*"

Barely stifling a giggle in time—she did not want to think about Ms. Letty watching a show like *SATC*—Madeline nodded and scooted forward in her chair. With the warm buzz of wine flowing through her veins and a friendly, eager listener at her disposal, she launched into a tour-guide-worthy conversation about her home city. The older woman asked questions, laughed at the appropriate times, and lit up with delight at several of Madeline's descriptions. It was everything she hadn't realized she needed.

"Well, my goodness, what are you two chattering on about?" Laurie Beth stood smiling in the doorway, her hands full of foil-wrapped leftovers.

Ms. Letty chuckled as she patted Madeline's hand. "Ms. Harper here was just regaling me with stories from the city. I'm green with envy from this girl's storytelling. Tickled pink, too!"

Laurie Beth smiled and leaned down to brush a kiss on the older woman's cheek before straightening. "That's sweet. Well, I'm fixin' to head out. Do you want to follow me, Ms. Harper?"

"Oh, I probably should. I'll get lost otherwise."

"Nonsense, dear," Ms. Letty said, tightening her grip on Madeline's fingers. "I've got directions printed up around here somewhere, so there's no rush. Besides, I may have plied you with a bit too much of that wine for you to be rushing off just yet."

Madeline conceded the wisdom of that with a nod, even though she'd only had two glasses of wine over the past two and a half hours. She bade good-bye to Laurie Beth before turning back to her host.

"I think I did all the talking tonight, I'm sorry to say. It was wonderful to talk with you, though. You should come visit me in the city when I go back."

Her penciled-in eyebrows rose. "You're going back? But you just moved here!" She seemed genuinely dismayed.

Madeline smiled gently. "And I'm happy to be here, but this is only a temporary move."

When the older woman chuckled, Madeline raised her brows in question. "I think I said the same thing forty years ago before I married my husband. I was from San Antonio and couldn't imagine living in the wilderness like this."

"Oh?" Madeline said, surprised to learn she wasn't a native of the town. "What changed your mind?"

"I loved my man, and my man loved this land. I don't know when it happened, but somewhere along the way I fell in love with the land, too." Her pale-blue eyes were wistful as she seemed to look into the past. "Funny how things like that sneak up."

Nodding, Madeline smiled. "I'm glad it worked out for the best for you." She stifled a yawn and glanced at the clock. It was almost nine thirty. Pushing away from the table, she rose and said, "Let me help you clean up a bit before I go."

Ms. Letty started to answer, but the sound of the back door opening had her hopping out of her chair. "Oh, good, that must be my grandson."

Madeline had done so much of the talking, she hadn't even asked the woman about her family. She'd have to make an effort to meet up with her again so they could talk more about her life next time.

Pasting a polite smile on her face, Madeline turned to greet the boy, but immediately froze when her eyes locked with the tall, broad, *very* familiar man who walked through the door.

"Ah, Tanner," the older woman exclaimed, delight brightening her voice. "Do I have someone to introduce to you."

# Chapter 11

TANNER STOOD AS rigid as a stone statue as, for the space of a few seconds, his brain galloped straight to the worst-case scenario. Lord help him—and *her*—if Madeline had aired their dirty laundry to his sharp-as-a-tack, old-fashioned grandmother.

But his logic caught up to his racing thoughts a few heart-beats later. Based on Grandma Letty's cheerful greeting, nothing had been said…yet.

Thank God.

He took a deep breath and forced a tight grin as he tipped his head in greeting toward the women. His grandmother's overly enthusiastic welcome registered at last. Cautiously, he said, "Is that so?"

She looked perfectly innocent as she hurried over to give him a hug, but he knew a matchmaking smile when he saw one, and this one had Cupid written all over it. He almost snorted. As if he needed any more encouragement to make a fool out of himself in front of Madeline.

He allowed his gaze to stray back to the "someone" in question. The mere sight of her standing there when he walked in the door had knocked the air straight from his lungs. What in the world was she doing here in his family's home, looking sexy sweet in her pink jeans and lacy white shirt? He was still mad at her, no matter how cute she looked.

"Yes, sir," Grandma Letty replied, with a devilish twinkle in her blue eyes. She swept a beckoning hand toward their visitor. "Miss Madeline, you must meet my handsome grandson. He's practically famous, believe it or not."

When his eyes collided with Madeline's, he mentally implored her to keep her mouth shut about any of their time together. Hell, he'd rather his grandmother not suspect they even knew each other. One whiff of a connection and she was liable to run with it like a dog with a stolen T-bone.

Madeline's expression was unreadable, and that made his pulse quicken. But after only a few seconds, she slid her gaze over to his grandmother and smiled. "You must be very proud to have a famous grandson."

Tanner's rigid shoulders relaxed. She was clever—there was no lie in her response. His grandmother fairly preened as she nodded and patted his arm. "Proud as a peacock. Well, now that he's retired," she added. "Leave it to a man to make a career out of riding an ornery beast ten times his weight. This old heart of mine couldn't have taken much more."

For the first time in years, guilt pricked his conscience over the matter. It had taken his grandmother years to not visibly pale anytime someone mentioned the rodeo, but toward the end of his career, they had come to a cease-fire over the matter. She'd even shown up for his last competition. He didn't want to think on the worry he'd caused her by chasing his dream.

Now, following the last conversation he'd had with Madeline about his choice of career, he felt the old defensiveness set in. The way she was looking at him, with one brow raised in an I-told-you-it-was-crazy sort of way, got his dander up all over again.

Pointedly turning his attention away from her golden gaze, he squeezed his grandmother's hand. "I reckon you'll outlive us all, no matter what I do for a living."

"We'll leave that up to the good Lord, thank you. I'm just glad to have you back home where you belong." She turned a smile toward their visitor. "And speaking of home, Madeline is new to town. Now mind your manners and greet her proper-like."

He suppressed a sigh. There was no escaping now that he was here. Stepping forward, he held out a hand. "Nice of you to come visit, Madeline."

She glanced down at his hand, looking distinctly surprised by the gesture. After a second, she reached out and slid her hand into his. "Glad to be here, Tanner. Your grandmother is a delight."

The feel of her soft, warm skin against his work-roughened palms sent a spark of desire through him. It wasn't a welcome sensation, given how they'd last parted. They were all wrong for each other, no matter what his thumping heart had to say about the matter. He quickly broke contact and shoved his hand in his pockets.

"Well, I won't keep you," he said pointedly.

"Oh, um, I was just about to help clean up," she replied, shooting a look toward his grandmother. "What can I do?"

"Why don't you gather up the wineglasses while I sit a spell? Tanner here can do the washing."

His jaw nearly hit the floor. In all his years, he'd never once seen his grandmother accept a guest's offer to clean up. Hell, she'd barely ever accepted his! And here she was, not only shamelessly accepting Madeline's offer, but enlisting Tanner after his nearly twelve-hour workday out in the barn.

Oh, yes, Grandma Letty was definitely in the matchmaking business tonight.

He opened his mouth to say he'd take care of it all, but Madeline beat him to the punch. "Absolutely. Now go relax. Your grandson and I will take care of everything."

Madeline had seen exactly what Tanner was about to say, and she wasn't going to let it happen. It seemed best to cut him off before he could protest. Her conscience demanded that she apologize for her mean words, and this was probably the best place for it. She didn't want things to get out of hand between them—as things tended to do when Tanner was involved—

and standing in his grandmother's kitchen seemed a good place to clear the air.

Ms. Letty smiled wide, patted her hand in thanks, and made a beeline for the living room. She turned on the television, cranking it up loud enough for Madeline to know for certain she was trying to afford them some privacy.

Turning back to the woman's scowling grandson, she said, "I'm happy to do the washing, if you'd prefer."

"I can handle it," he said brusquely. He went to the sink and turned on the water.

She hesitated for a moment before going about gathering up all the used wineglasses. When she set them on the countertop near his elbow, she turned so she could look up at him. "I didn't know this was your grandparents' house."

She couldn't say why, but it felt important that he know that this wasn't some sort of conspiracy. That was obviously what he thought, at least initially. The moment he'd locked eyes with her, his expression had conveyed nothing short of horror, as though she was specifically there to divulge every detail of their relationship so far.

He grabbed the closest glass and plunged it in the soapy water. "Just randomly showed up at a stranger's house for a good time, huh?"

"Laurie Beth Simmons invited me to her book club. How was I supposed to know your grandmother would be hosting?"

He sent her a sidelong glance, reluctant amusement lifting

his lips. "Ah, Laurie Beth. That girl could find trouble blind-folded. How'd you get mixed up with her?"

The momentary flash of jealousy at the fondness his voice betrayed surprised her. *Ridiculous*. He was free to be fond of whomever he liked. Besides, she liked her assistant, impertinent as she could sometimes be. "She works for me. In fact," she added, attempting to lighten his mood, "she's the one who informed me of your heartthrob status."

He shook his head as he soaped up another wineglass. "She always was well informed," he deadpanned.

Finally—a bit of his normal teasing self. It was the opening she was waiting for. Bumping his hip with hers, she smiled up at him. "Hey, you. I'm sorry about the things I said to you before. I was a total jerk, and you didn't deserve it."

Tanner slowed in his scrubbing and tossed another look her way. "You know, my mama and grandma taught me to never argue with a woman. In the interest of good manners, I'll agree with you on the matter."

Chuckling, Madeline shook her head. "I see. Well, thank you. I think."

He rinsed the glass and shook the water from his fingers before turning to face her, one hand resting lightly at his hip. "In the interest of fairness, I admit I acted like an ass that night, too."

"Did you?" she asked, teasing him in spite of herself. "I can't say I noticed a difference from your normal person-ality."

That elicited a laugh. He playfully flicked water at her. "Damn Yankee," he growled lightly.

She squeaked and jumped back. "Hey! I happen to like this shirt."

His grin was slow and sexy as his gaze dropped to the lacy top. "What a coincidence. So do I."

Awareness rushed through her veins. Pretending her heart hadn't just stuttered a bit, she lifted an eyebrow and pointed at the sink. "Eyes on the dishes, buddy. You're not leaving me with this mess."

He shot her a rueful glance. "And by 'this' mess do you mean *your* mess? God knows my beverage of choice is not served in a wineglass. I'm just helping you out of the goodness of my heart."

"Mmhmm. More like out of fear of your grandmother."

"No shame in that," he said easily. "That woman put the fear of God into me when I was a kid. I haven't forgotten it, and neither has my butt."

She bit her lip against a laugh. The last thing she needed to be reminded of was his backside. Seriously, though, his voice held so much fondness when he spoke of his grandmother, even Madeline's heart tugged. Whatever anyone could say about Tanner, he certainly loved his family.

The back door opened then, and a tall, thin man with tan, weathered skin and bright-white hair poking out from under a cowboy hat walked in. He came up short as his clear blue gaze landed on Madeline. "Well, howdy," he said, his voice a gravelly version of Tanner's. He quickly pulled off his hat and tossed it on the table. "I expected to find a pretty lady in my kitchen, but you're about four decades younger than the lady I had in mind."

"Jack? Is that you?" Ms. Letty's voice called out from the living room. "You leave the young people be and come sit in here."

"Hold your horses, woman," he called back, winking to Madeline. Lowering his voice, he said, "Aren't you gonna introduce me, Tanner?"

"Sure thing," Tanner said mildly. "This here is Miss Madeline Harper, recently relocated from New York City. Madeline, my grandfather, Jackson Callen, better known as Grandpa Jack."

Thrusting out her hand in greeting, Madeline smiled. "So nice to meet you, sir. I've enjoyed a lovely evening with your wife."

His hand was calloused and leathery, but still warm and gentle. "Pleasure to meet you, Miss Madeline. I hope Tanner here isn't giving you any trouble."

She sent a teasing glance toward the troublemaker in question. "Not today, anyway."

She realized she'd implied they'd met before when the older man's white eyebrows rose with interest. He opened his mouth to respond, but his wife chose that minute to yell for him again.

Shaking his head, he said, "I know better than to keep my

bride waiting. Now don't you worry yourself about cleaning up. That's what the help's for," he said with a teasing nod toward Tanner. With a smile to Madeline and a firm *thwack* to Tanner's back, Jack made his way to the living room.

Crossing his arms, Tanner sent her a wry half grin. "I guess you're off the hook. Better get while the gettin's good."

The idea of heading home wasn't nearly as appealing as it should have been. Sighing, she nodded. "Probably a good idea. Your grandmother mentioned something about printed directions?"

"Sure. Just give me a minute to rustle them up." He wiped his hands on a faded yellow-and-white dish towel before disappearing into the hallway.

Within minutes Madeline had said her good-byes, been smothered by Ms. Letty's hug for the second time that night, and agreed to see the woman again soon. By then, Tanner was waiting with the directions in hand at the front door.

"Dark night," he said, his voice soft and quiet. "I'll walk you to your car."

Another night, she might have turned him down. But tonight his gaze was warm, the night chilly, and the property unfamiliar. She could feel the buzz of electricity sparking to life again between them, and she wasn't ready to turn her back on that just yet.

She wet her lips and nodded, ignoring the dull voice of reason in the back of her head. "After you."

# Chapter 12

BEFORE STEPPING OUT onto the porch, Tanner reached for Madeline's hand, and for once, she didn't protest. It was dark, after all. And gravel never mixed well with heels. And all sorts of wild animals lived in Texas.

And she wanted to hold his hand.

There, she admitted it. Sometimes a woman just wanted to hold a man's hand. It didn't hurt that Tanner was pretty much the definition of the word *hot*.

They strolled to her car lazily, as if they were wandering through a park. In the darkness, it was natural to savor the warmth of his hand and the firm length of his muscled arm against hers. The faint hint of his cologne traveled on the crisp night air, reminding her of the first night they had spent together. She swallowed, trying to be her normal sensible self but drifting closer to him with every step.

When they reached her car, neither of them made a move to open the door. The night was so quiet, she could hear when he drew in a long, slow breath as his thumb caressed her hand.

"Have you looked up since coming here?" he asked, his voice a gruff whisper.

She tilted her chin back, but her gaze didn't travel any farther than the darkened planes of his handsome face. "New Yorkers don't look up," she said, her voice oddly breathy.

"I guarantee you'll never see a sky so big anywhere else. Take a step outside of that box of yours and see what you're missing."

She already saw what she was missing. He was right in front of her, with tousled brown hair and eyes that betrayed his every thought. Why did they have to feel so *right* together? All logic said that they were incompatible, but here she was, feeling like she was exactly where she should be.

His lips tugged into a soft grin. Reaching up, he gently put a finger beneath her chin and tilted her head up.

Letting go of her conflicting emotions, she allowed her gaze to shift. The sky above them didn't look real. It was like one of those enhanced satellite pictures of the Milky Way, with swirls of stars scattered like pixie dust across an indigo carpet. She breathed an appreciative sigh, as aware of the warmth of his touch as she was of the spectacular view of the heavens. "Incredible."

He shifted, leaning back against the car and pulling her gently against him. "My thoughts exactly."

Her heart kick-started in her chest. She knew he wasn't talking about the view. When she dropped her gaze to his, he was watching her with a look that made her stomach flip. "I really should go," she said softly, but didn't move an inch.

"Yes, you should," he murmured, but kept his place, too.

"I have work tomorrow." She leaned the slightest bit forward, just enough that her hips met his, and her breasts grazed his broad chest.

"I'm sure you do." His fingers tightened on her waist, sending a shiver down her spine. Slowly, deliberately, he pulled her more firmly against him. "So let me kiss you good-night."

Tanner's heart pounded as he waited for her to answer. He wanted her—God, did he want her—but he didn't want any misunderstandings between them. Their relationship so far had been about as predictable as a tornado in December.

He loved the feel of her in his arms. His fingers brushed over the bare skin of her lower back, just under the hem of her shirt. It was impossible not to think of the night he had touched that same spot with his lips.

"I don't know that we should," she whispered, leaning in so close that he could feel the warmth of her breath across his cheek.

"I do. We *definitely* should."

It was all he could do to hold still, to wait for her to make her decision. After a few suspenseful heartbeats, she smiled softly and said, "Maybe just this once."

*Thank God.* Not waiting another second, he wrapped his

arms fully around her waist and pressed his lips to hers. The soft sound of satisfaction she made went right through him. He hadn't forgotten how well they fit together, how perfectly their bodies melted into each other.

He kissed her long and slow beneath the great big Texas sky. He took his time exploring, not wanting to rush a single moment. If she was giving him just this once, he would take the opportunity to change her mind. Because this kind of chemistry? It didn't come along every day.

He nibbled, he caressed, his tongue tangled with hers again and again. And it felt so damn good. So *right*. They seemed to have the whole world to themselves.

It was several long minutes before she pulled away and looked up at him with those big eyes of hers. Despite the dim light, he could still see a glimmer of gold in their depths.

Licking her kiss-swollen bottom lip, she said, "I should go."

He smiled. "Yeah, we established that already."

She laughed softly and shook her head. "Right. Well, this time I mean it." Looking back up to him, she gave him a little half smile. "Thanks for seeing me out. I'll…talk to you later."

He kissed her one last time, short and sweet, before she got into that fancy car of hers and took off. As she drove away, he was struck by how amazing she really was. She was brave enough to move halfway across the country on her own, to step into an intimidating job (though she'd played it down), and to make the most of an area she disliked by joining a book club and befriending an old woman.

He never intended for her to meet his family. None of the women he dated ever even saw his hometown, because he'd laid down ground rules on the subject years ago. But the thing was, weren't rules made to be broken?

In this case, he was beginning to think they were.

## Chapter 13

MADELINE HAD JUST taken a bite of her apple, feta, and pecan salad when her cellphone buzzed. Looking away from the spreadsheet she was studying—the terse email from corporate this morning had deemed the review a priority—she peered at the number on the display. It didn't look familiar, but the area code was local.

She hesitated to answer, but very few people in the area had her cell number. Curiosity getting the better of her, she quickly swallowed her bite and picked up the phone. "This is Madeline," she said briskly.

"I was hoping I would catch you on your lunch break. How'd I do?"

Her stomach did a little somersault at the sound of Tanner's unmistakable drawl. She'd dreamed about their kiss last night, but she wasn't sure that the dream version was any better than the real thing. "I'm taking a working lunch. How did you get my number?"

"Believe it or not, my grandmother texted it to me this morning. 'Just in case,' it said."

Madeline laughed lightly. "Your grandmother texts?"

It was hard to picture Ms. Letty sitting in her 1970s wood-paneled kitchen, tapping away on a cellphone. Heck, the harvest-gold phone mounted to the wall was an honest-to-God rotary.

"You better believe it. She discovered she was much more likely to hear from me if she texted when I was on the circuit."

She didn't even try to stifle the grin that came to her lips. "So your grandmother is more tech-savvy than you, huh?"

"Hey, now. Grandma Letty's got me licked on a lot of things, but technology is definitely not one of them."

"And yet you actually *called* me. I can't remember the last time I willingly talked to someone on the phone outside of work. It's *so* two thousand and seven," she teased.

The deep rumble of his laughter made her heart lift. "Would you hang up on me if I told you I'd wanted to hear your voice?"

She bit her lip. "I should."

"Mmhmm. I don't hear a click," he said. She could actually hear the smile in his voice.

She glanced down to the spreadsheet in front of her and sighed. Now was not the time to be bantering with the man. "What is it that you want, Tanner? I am a busy woman, you know." She rustled the papers on her desk for effect.

"You." He paused just long enough to make her wonder. "I've decided it's high time you saw God's country the way it was intended."

"And how is that?" she asked suspiciously.

"Come on by my place tomorrow at ten and find out."

"That's way too vague for me to drop everything and come all the way out there."

"Is it?" he drawled. "And here I was hoping it'd be just vague enough to pique your interest. I guess we'll find out tomorrow." And just like that, he said good-bye and hung up the phone.

She stared at the display in disbelief. His confidence was astounding. Let him hope whatever he wanted. Madeline was most definitely not going over there tomorrow.

He was waiting for her when she pulled up at five after ten the next morning.

Alright, so he had been right about her curiosity, but she refused to let him gloat about it. Besides, it was a Saturday and she had nothing else planned, and yesterday had turned out to be a super-rough day. Tanner was her escape, whether she admitted it or not.

Turning the engine off, she stepped out of the car and set a hand to her hip. "This had better be good."

She lifted an eyebrow in expectant challenge, even as she drank in the sight of him in his faded plaid shirt with the sleeves rolled up, and those perfect-fitting jeans that he loved so much. He looked like the lead in a modern cowboy movie. It was a look she was rapidly growing fond of.

His smile was slow and wide, making his eyes crinkle at

the corners. He tugged at the brim of his hat and said, "Yes, ma'am, it will be. Follow me."

He led her toward the barn, his boots crunching loudly on the gravel underfoot. As they stepped through the wide doorway into the darkness, the smell of horses and hay assailed her senses. There were several stalls, and two horses clipped to a pair of leads in the main corridor.

Madeline came to an abrupt halt, realization dawning. "What, exactly, do you have planned, Tanner? I assumed you were planning to take me on a tour of the county's backcountry."

He nodded as he walked to the nearest horse, a slender but tall reddish-brown mare. "That's right. On the back of a horse, as God intended." He picked up a saddle and heaved it onto the beast.

Her eyes went wide as she took a quick step backward. "Are you crazy?" It was one thing to ride in a horse-drawn carriage in Central Park; it was another to actually sit on top of a horse.

"For you, maybe," he said with a grin over his shoulder as he cinched a leather strap tight. "But when it comes to horses, darlin', I don't mess around."

She shook her head in disbelief. Didn't he tell her just days ago that his father had been killed while riding? "You're not just crazy; you're certifiable. I'm not getting on the back of that thing."

The animal was truly beautiful, and it waited very patiently while Tanner messed with the saddle. But that didn't make Madeline any more inclined to climb on its back.

He finished securing it in place before turning to her with a look that was somehow both chiding and challenging. "Live a little, Madeline. I promise you'll enjoy it, once you learn to ride." He was gently coaxing, with that crooked smile tilting his lips. "People always fear the unknown."

"I *do* want to live, which is why I'm not getting on a huge, muscular beast with its multiple sharp hooves."

He patted the horse's neck. "Miss Red here is as gentle as a new mama. You can trust me on that."

No. He was nuts, and she wouldn't do this. Even though his voice was warm and tempting and his earnestness seemed genuine, she couldn't take the risk.

She bit her lip. *Could she?*

"Give me two hours," he said, sensing her hesitation. "We can ride to the river for a picnic. If you don't like it, we'll be close enough to walk back."

"Tanner—" she said, about to refuse, but he stepped forward and set his hands on her upper arms, looking her straight in the eyes.

"Trust me, Maddie. And don't worry; it's not a date. I'll be sure to charge you for the lesson when we get back."

Laughing, she shook her head. "You're impossible."

She didn't even complain at the shortening of her name. Her parents had made sure no one ever tried to "bastardize" her name, as they called it, but she liked the way it rolled off his tongue. She liked the way *everything* rolled off his tongue.

"I am," he said with an unrepentant grin. "Now say you'll ride with me."

She drew a deep breath, scrunched her nose, and nodded. She might be crazy—she was about to put her life in the hands of a cowboy and his horse. And, no, she didn't want to examine her reasons too carefully.

# Chapter 14

"YOU LIED TO ME."

Tanner raised an eyebrow at Madeline, playing innocent. "I don't know what you're talking about."

She threw him a mock-disgruntled look even as a smile tugged at the corners of her mouth. She looked so damn cute, perched on top of Miss Red in her washed-out jeans and ball cap, her tennis-shoed feet poking through the stirrups. "This has to be miles from your house. It'd be impossible to walk back."

Grinning, he said, "Technically, any distance is walkable if you want it bad enough." He laughed when she made a show of rolling her eyes at him. "Besides, I knew you wouldn't want to walk once you gave this a try, and I was right. You look like you were born to ride horses."

She snorted. "Hardly. My hands ache from clutching the reins so hard for so long. And we're not even going to talk about what else is aching."

He gave a short bark of laughter. Pulling up on the reins,

he brought his horse to a stop and dismounted. He looped the reins over the saddle horn before clipping the tethered rope he'd installed years ago to Levi's bridle. The river gurgled pleasantly a few yards away, its surface glittering in the late morning sun. This had always been his favorite spot. He was looking forward to sharing it with someone else for the first time.

Walking over to Madeline's side, he grabbed Miss Red's reins and said, "But you *have* enjoyed it."

It had looked to him like Madeline had settled in after about ten minutes, with her body relaxing and rolling with the mare's easy gait. Her burgeoning confidence was both endearing and adorable.

She was the kind of woman who liked to be in control of herself and her surroundings, and her willingness to trust him with this made him think there might be hope for the two of them yet.

Sending him a reluctant smile, she nodded. "It's been surprisingly nice. It really is beautiful out here."

Looking up at her with wide eyes, he said, "I don't believe it. Was that an actual compliment for my hometown?"

One slender blond eyebrow lifted beneath the brim of her hat. "If I say yes, will you get me off this horse?"

Chuckling, he showed her where to put her hands to hold herself steady as she dismounted. "Pull both feet clear of the stirrups, swing your leg around, then slide on down."

She looked down at him anxiously. "What if the horse spooks? Or if I slip?"

"I've got the reins, so she's not going anywhere. And I'll be right here to catch you no matter what."

Nodding, she followed his instructions. He got a mighty fine view of her backside as she swung her leg around and dangled for a second.

He put his arm around her waist to lighten the pressure on the horse's back. "I got you. You can let go."

To his surprise, she immediately complied. She slid against him in a controlled fall until her feet touched the ground at last. He tossed the reins over the saddle horn, trusting Miss Red to stay put, but left his other hand right where it was, resting at the top of Madeline's hip.

"You did good," he murmured, his lips at her ear. She smelled good, too. The fruity scent of her shampoo mixed well with the fresh Texas air. He bent his head to nuzzle her neck. Her skin was soft and sweet and so inviting, it was all he could do not to nip the tempting little spot at the junction of her shoulder. She leaned into him for all of three seconds before suddenly straightening and turning in his arms.

"Oh, no," she said, her cheeks flushed but her chin tipped up in determination. "I was promised a picnic lunch, and I will not be sidetracked, thank you very much."

He stepped back and wagged his eyebrows. "Maybe for dessert, then. But come on, I've got a top-notch meal packed for us." He nodded toward Levi and went to fetch the grub.

She followed along behind him. "Top-notch, huh? Got some orecchiette with rapini and goat cheese in there? Herbed frittatas?"

Grinning at her teasing, he spread out the blanket. "Better than that," he said as he reached into the bag. With a great flourish, he revealed its contents. "Only the best for you, Maddie."

Madeline laughed out loud when she saw his offering. "Peanut butter and jelly sandwiches?"

He nodded as he handed one over, an adorable yet sexy grin teasing his lips. "Peanut butter with homemade strawberry jam on the finest white bread sold in all of Harvey's General Store.

"And," he added as he reached into the satchel again, "cucumber salad made by yours truly, and Grandma Letty's famous mac and cheese, good even when cold. She swears the extra ingredient is love, but I have it on good authority that it's actually just double butter and cheese."

Even as she laughed, she was genuinely touched by the gesture. He'd remembered her vegetarianism, and he'd obviously taken care when packing the meal. Nodding in approval, she said, "A gourmet feast if I've ever seen one."

She sat back and watched as he filled two plastic plates. The soft breeze ruffled his hair as he concentrated on his task. The horses grazed contentedly near the riverbank—which was more of a stream bank, if you asked her—and the tree above them provided just enough shade for her to take off her hat and shake out her hair.

"This is nice," she said when he handed over her plate. "I like the noise of the stream. It takes the edge off the quiet in this part of the country."

"Hmm," he replied, eyeing her as he took a bite of his sandwich, "I'm not sure I've ever thought the quiet was something that needed changin'."

"It's what you're used to." She wondered what he would think of New York City if he ever came to stay for a while. The thought was so unexpected, she dropped her eyes and concentrated on her sandwich. Is that what she wanted? For her time here to bleed into her real life someday?

"It's what I like," he clarified. "I haven't been to the Northeast, but I've been to plenty of cities. I think some people crave the quiet, and some people crave the noise." He flashed her a smile that sent a flutter through her belly. "Although I was really hoping the quiet—and Sunnybell— would grow on you."

"I'll admit, I'm beginning to appreciate some of its charms. I still like skyscrapers and taxis more than scrubby grassland and horses, but"—she shrugged, looking around at the rolling Texas hills—"like I said, it's nice. Peaceful, but nice."

He laughed and shook his head. "Only you would add a 'but' to that sentence."

"Just being honest."

Holding up his fork as a salute, he said, "I admire honesty. Grandpa Jack always says it's the trickiest virtue of all. It's all in how you wield it."

She tilted her head. "He seems like a good man. In fact, I remember you saying he saved your life." She was prying, and she knew it, but it wasn't the first time she'd wondered over the words.

He nodded solemnly as he chewed a forkful of the pasta. "I was…reckless for a few years there when I was a teenager. My mother struggled with raising me alone, and I was still mad about losing my father. I acted out in ways I'm not proud of. Got involved with people I shouldn't have. Grandpa Jack took me in hand."

He didn't seem to mind talking about it, so she decided to press on. "Oh? How so?"

"Gave me direction and guidance. Discipline. He showed me the meaning of hard work and gave me an outlet for my wildness. Grandma Letty hated the risks I took in the rodeo, but my grandfather knew they were a hell of a lot better than the alternative."

The warmth and respect that flooded his voice when he spoke of either of his grandparents was unmistakable. She smiled softly at him, drawing her knees up to her chest. She envied him and the relationship he shared with his grandparents. His grandparents delighted in his presence. Her parents considered weekly phone calls just a little too clingy. They'd congratulated themselves on a job well done when they'd raised her to sprout wings strong enough to never have to return to the nest.

"You're lucky, you know that?"

"I do," he said with a single nod. Setting down his plate, he slid over closer to her. "Luckier still for having caught you with your guard down that first night."

"Hey, I'm not defensive," she said defensively. When he laughed, she relented. "I'm protective, not defensive. I don't want to mess up my life."

He reached out to tuck a lock of hair behind her ear. "Nah, you'll never do that. You're much too smart."

"Oh, really? If I'm so smart, what the heck am I doing out here?"

What *was* she doing, sitting beside him in the middle of nowhere, getting lost in his Tiffany eyes and lazy drawl? She should be at work, figuring out what was bothering her about the documents she had reviewed yesterday.

He slid the back of his fingers down the bare skin of her arm. "Life can't all be about what your brain says. Sometimes you have to listen to your heart, too."

"That doesn't sound very prudent," she said, even as she watched the path his fingers took over her skin.

He leaned forward until his lips were just above hers. "That's because you're thinking too much."

And then his lips were on hers, and she wasn't thinking about anything at all. She allowed him to slowly push her down onto the blanket, teasing her with his tongue and lips all the while. He braced himself with his left arm, the muscles flexing enticingly, while his right hand explored the curve of her hip. She exhaled with pleasure when his lips found the base of her neck.

Taking full advantage of the position, she slid her hands over the hard wall of his abdomen. She reveled in the rippled plane, groaning as she remembered gliding against him, skin to skin, less than two weeks ago. After a minute, her hand continued upward, traveling across his rock-solid chest before slipping along the hard knot of his biceps. She squeezed, her fingers digging lightly into his taut skin.

With a growl, he found her lips again and kissed her deeply.

*Yes, please!* She arched up as his palm slipped up her rib cage and settled over her breast. The warmth of his hand was absolute heaven. He kneaded gently even as his tongue tangled hotly with hers.

Their night together was supposed to be a one-time thing—no, it *would* be a one-time thing—but how could she resist this? He was a hot, willing cowboy with a sense of humor and a killer body, and he clearly wanted her as much as she did him. And, Lord, did she want him. When he pulled away again to trail kisses along the curve of her jaw, she sighed with bliss.

"I like you, Maddie," he whispered against her kiss-dampened skin. "A whole hell of a lot." He pulled back just enough to look her in the eye, squeezing her waist gently as he did. "And I don't have to think about it to know we go to-gether like bees and honey."

He was simplifying the issue, but she'd have plenty of time to think about it later. Right now, all she wanted to do was get lost in his incredible kisses. She reached up and clasped her hands behind the back of his neck and pulled him back down for more. Then, just as their lips were about to meet, her phone buzzed in her back pocket, jarring her out of the moment.

It was all the more jarring when she realized it hadn't made a peep since they left his house.

Dragging in a deep breath, she tried to clear her fuzzy brain. The man was like a drug. "Hang on, I should get that," she said, pushing on his shoulders.

He closed his eyes for a moment before saying, "You sure you want to get that? Nobody expects you to respond to a text right that second. Defeats the purpose, doesn't it?"

She wasn't sure she wanted to deal with it, but it was too late now. Reason was pushing back against the mental road-blocks she'd set up. *Crap.* Smiling apologetically, she nodded.

He sighed and reluctantly pushed himself into a sitting position before helping her up. He looked disheveled and flustered and sexy as hell, but she forced herself to look away to pull out her phone.

"I can't believe I got any signal out here," she said as the screen pulled up.

Shrugging, he sat back and plucked a blade of grass. "Calls

never come through, but texts eventually make their way, given enough time."

As she read the message, disbelief turned her blood to ice. "Oh, God," she said, rereading the message again. Alarm raced through her as she scrambled to her feet.

"What is it?" Tanner asked, his brow creased with concern as he stood.

"I have to go. Right now." She swallowed and looked up at him, her heart thundering and her mind already miles away from where they stood. "The deal just fell through."

## *Chapter 15*

THE ALL-CAPS TEXT message that Madeline received from her boss back at corporate may as well have been tattooed to the back of her eyelids.

WESTERFIELD HAS BROKEN THE CONTRACT. WHERE ARE YOU?

Where had she been when they'd called her a dozen times and sent no fewer than six emails? She'd been staring moony-eyed at a sweet-talking cowboy with a lazy smile and way-too-kissable lips. She'd been a million miles away indulging a fantasy that she knew was off-limits.

The whole ride home, she cursed the decision to ride horseback, wishing she could spur the horse into a gallop, but too damn afraid to despite the dire circumstances. It was almost two hours before she reached the office and learned exactly what had happened.

How had she missed the signs? How had she not seen that Westerfield was getting cold feet about giving up his life's work to a cold corporate entity thousands of miles away?

She'd worked hard for weeks, for God's sake! She'd been so damn cocky that she had everything under control, but really Westerfield was just humoring her, all the while quietly undermining the entire deal.

Her day was utterly hellacious after that. Call after call, dozens of pages of legal documents, months of work raked over with a fine-tooth comb. There was nothing anyone could find that showed that she had done something wrong, and yet...

The buck stopped with her.

She'd failed to see the merger through to completion. It didn't matter that Westerfield had exploited a loophole that the legal team should have buttoned up in the contract. It didn't matter that that particular part of the deal had been worked on prior to her taking over. She was the acquisitions manager, and she had somehow managed to *un*acquire the one project she was in charge of.

It was after nine when she finally dragged herself home, numb and hollow. She felt she'd hardly slept ten minutes when her phone rang the next morning. The red letters of her clock read seven twenty-one as she jerked upright and grabbed it before it went to voicemail. She grimaced when she saw her boss's name flash across the screen. Straightening her shoulders in an effort to shake off her exhaustion, she accepted the call and pressed the phone to her ear. "This is Madeline."

"Madeline, it's Franklin. Sorry to call so early on a Sunday morning, but I wanted to catch you before you went in."

"No, no, it's fine," she said, trying to smooth the sleep-roughened quality of her voice.

"Listen, the company has accepted that this is a total loss situation, and, well, I don't want to drag this out for you."

It wasn't an unexpected call. The company wouldn't want to waste another dollar by having her remain down here in Texas when the deal was dead. "I understand completely, sir. I can be back at corporate by Wednesday."

It would be brutal, packing up and driving all the way back in less than three days, but she wasn't about to appear lax after this whole disaster. She had a feeling she was going to be making up for this black mark on her record for years to come.

There was a beat of silence on the other end that made the hair at the back of her neck stand on end. In those two seconds, dread washed over her.

"The point is," Franklin said hesitantly, "I'm afraid your current position has been made redundant with this deal falling through."

She blinked, trying to digest the words. "I…I see. Well, that makes sense, I suppose. If the company feels I should step down to my old assistant position again, I will of course do so."

A demotion was almost unthinkable, but she could work her way back up eventually. The promotion had been practically a fluke, anyway. It would be a bitter blow to her pride, but she could handle it.

She closed her eyes, trying not to think of her parents' reaction to the news.

"No, Madeline. The thing is, the CFO's nephew has settled in rather well in your old position. Mr. Kennedy intends for Jeremy to continue." He paused, and she could almost hear him swallow. "I regret to inform you that with the company's changing needs, we are going to have to let you go."

It took less than three hours to pack up her things in her rental house. She'd never intended to stay for very long, after all—so much of her stuff was still in storage in New York. On Monday, she called the moving company and scheduled a time for them to pick everything up, informed the property management company of her intention to break the lease, and got in touch with the receptionist to meet her at the office before heading in.

She didn't want to see Laurie Beth, or Westerfield, or any of the people she had worked with. She was an utter failure, and the thought of seeing the pity in their eyes was too much to bear. Mrs. McLeroy was the only one she could think of who would be professional and somewhat discreet. She was also the only one who'd never given her a knowing glance when it came to Tanner.

Tanner.

She couldn't even think about him right now. Her heart was already fractured—she didn't need the added stress of dealing with him. She'd been so stupid to get caught up with him in the first place. What had she thought would happen? That she could have a fling with a local while biding her time here? She'd let herself get carried away when she should have been 100 percent focused on her work.

It didn't matter now. She'd continue to ignore his texts until she was safe and sound back in New York. Then she'd send a note apologizing for the delay, and wishing him a nice life.

"Well, I hate to see you go, Ms. Harper," Mrs. McLeroy said with a kind smile as Madeline handed over her keys. "You may have felt like a square peg in a round hole at first, but I think we were just startin' to smooth out your corners."

Having no idea how to respond to that, Madeline just smiled politely. "Thank you, Mrs. McLeroy. And thank you again for agreeing to meet the movers later this week for me. That's a weight off my shoulders."

After nodding her good-bye, Madeline hoisted the last box and trudged out to the door, an odd reluctance settling in her chest. The last thing she expected to see as she headed to her car was Tanner leaning against her driver-side door, arms crossed and blue eyes thunderous.

She was too tired for this. Overwrought. Taking a fortifying breath, she nodded coolly before taking the box around to her passenger door and wedging it into the front seat. The rest of the car was already so full she might as well have had a brick wall in the back seat.

"Planning to leave without saying good-bye?" he said tightly, his voice accusing.

"I've got a lot on my mind. I was going to text you later." Too curious not to ask, she added, "How did you know I was here?"

"My buddy, Mack McLeroy, thought I might like to know his mother had headed to the office straight from church yesterday to help tie up some loose ends before you headed out of town." He shook his head, his eyes pinning her in place. "Heading back to your beloved New York without a word, huh?"

She came around to the driver's side, forced to confront him in order to get into her car. She didn't want to meet his eyes, to face the conversation coming, but there was no way to avoid it. "Yep," she said, purposely flippant. "Since I no longer have a job, I need to get back ASAP to start the job search."

His iciness gave way to something way too close to sympathy as he took a step toward her. "Aw, hell, Maddie—they fired you? That's ridiculous!" He sounded as outraged as she felt, not that it would do her a bit of good.

"They didn't so much fire me as declare my position redundant. Happens every day in corporate America," she said, with a shrug that didn't even begin to scratch the surface of her emotions on the issue.

She reached for the door handle, but he grabbed her hand, stopping her. "Then what's the hurry? If you aren't rushing back to a damn fool company that doesn't know a good thing when it has it, why not take a few days to figure things out?"

Closing her eyes against the familiar comfort of his hand on hers, she tugged away and backed up a step. "What's there to figure out?" she said briskly, steeling herself against the hurt in his eyes. "I need to get home so I can dive into the job market again. I have an excellent resume, and there are hundreds of jobs in the city that I'd be qualified for."

He shook his head. "But is that what you really want? Another job you don't care about at a nameless company that could just as easily sack you as keep you?"

She stiffened, angry that he managed to tap into the exact fear that had been rolling around inside her head all night. "I'm an excellent worker, thank you. My skill set is highly marketable, and I intend to use those skills to climb my way back up." This was a temporary bump in the road; she wouldn't let it derail her lifelong plans.

Blowing out a breath, Tanner ran a hand through his already mussed hair. "Damn it, I didn't mean to imply you weren't a stellar worker. But what do you really want to do with your life? Where is your *passion?*"

She shook her head, running away from the question. "I want success. A good nest egg. We talked about this already." Any doubts she had about the truth of that were merely because she was upset. It was natural, really. What person wouldn't be stung by the events of the last twenty-four hours?

"Maddie," he said softly, stepping forward and sliding his hands over her arms, "it doesn't have to be like that. You could stay, you know. Grandma Letty sure likes having you around, after all. I don't think your company's half bad, either," he teased gently.

No, she couldn't do this. She'd allowed herself to be distracted by him too much already, and look where that had gotten her. If she was going to succeed in piecing her life back together, she needed to focus. She'd already proven that when he was around, she couldn't even think straight.

Stepping backward very deliberately, she raised her chin and looked him in the eye. "My name is Madeline, not Maddie. And while it's been…*different* living here, I have to get back to my real life."

Even as she said the words, her heart ached fiercely, but she refused to back down. When she got home, everything would feel normal again.

He stared back at her, and for a moment, she thought he might argue. But then his lips pressed together and he nodded, stepping out of her way. "Well, Madeline, far be it from me to get in the way of your 'real life.' I sure hope you find what you're looking for."

With a tip of his hat, he turned and walked back to his truck, his boots tapping a crisp beat on the asphalt. Drawing a slow, steadying breath, she opened her door and slid into the soft leather driver seat. She started the car, backed out of the parking slot, and eventually turned east onto the highway. As the rolling hills of Sunnybell gradually receded in her rearview mirror, she focused only on the road ahead.

Soon she'd be home, and this too-quiet place and all the nosy people in it would be little more than a memory.

# Chapter 16

"YOU'RE KIDDING YOURSELF if you think your mama didn't raise no fools."

"Well, hello to you, too," Tanner said, dropping a kiss on his scowling grandmother's cheek. He and the hands had been riding fences all morning, and he was exhausted. It didn't help that he hadn't slept worth a damn the last few nights.

She rolled her eyes even as she handed him a tall glass of iced tea. "Lunch is on the table. And don't think you can change the subject. I've a bone to pick with you."

Settling into one of the kitchen chairs, he sighed and said, "What did I do this time?"

He honestly had no idea. He'd been working like a dog this past week in an effort to forget about the pretty little blonde who had swept in and out of his life like a hurricane. There were so many things he wished he'd said to her, but in the end, he doubted it would have mattered.

"After all these years, you finally meet your match, and you just let her waltz right out of your life without raising a whiff of protest."

His eyebrows inched up his forehead. "Meet my match? What are you talking about?" As far as Grandma Letty knew, he'd had little more than a passing acquaintance with Maddie.

*Madeline,* he mentally corrected.

Her hands went to her hips as she leveled an exasperated glare on him. "You must think I'm either blind or missing the sense God gave me, 'cause only a fool would miss the way you looked at that girl. And only a *stubborn* fool would miss the way she looked at you."

He just about choked on his tea. "What do you mean, the way she looked at me? You only saw her the one time."

It was clear from the get-go that he was much more invested than Madeline ever was. She was attracted to him, sure, but she saw him as nothing more than some sort of a diversion. A way to kill time until she could go back to New York.

His grandmother's face softened as she came to sit beside him. "I may be old, but I can spot love at a hundred paces. Plus, from what I heard, it sounded like you two really hit it off when you first met."

Her knowing look made him groan. Clearly the gossip had made its way to his grandmother's ears after all. "You weren't supposed to know that."

"And you weren't supposed to let her get away. But I suppose you got your stubbornness from me."

He sat back, digesting what she was saying. Truth was, he missed Madeline like crazy. He couldn't seem to let her go, and maybe it was because he didn't *want* to let her go. His heart lifted with what he recognized as hope as he considered what his grandmother had told him. Was it possible that Maddie really liked him as much as he cared about her? She'd seemed so distant when she left, but she had just been dealt an awful blow.

Sitting here in his grandmother's kitchen, it was impossible to know the answer to his question. A newfound resolve stiffened his back. He set down his glass and pushed to his feet. If he wanted to know if she felt the same way about him as he did about her, well, there was only one way to find out.

After all, that wasn't the sort of conversation a man had over the phone.

His first call was to the airline, which had a flight headed to LaGuardia at three. He didn't have a minute to waste. After a quick talk with Grandpa Jack—who grinned and told him to get the heck out of his barn and go get the girl—Tanner hopped in the truck and took off. Stopping only long enough to pack an overnight bag, he was on the highway in under half an hour.

From there he called Mack to ask him to look after the animals. His friend agreed after minimum ribbing. Next Tanner managed to sweet-talk Mack's mother into giving him Madeline's New York address, though she swore she'd have his hide if he divulged how he got it. Not that he was sure Madeline would actually be at that address. It was a long shot at best, but he'd cross that bridge once he got there.

When at last he made it to the airport, he parked his truck in the first spot he came to, slung his bag over his shoulder, and jogged for the entrance. This might be the craziest thing he'd ever done, but he knew better than anyone that if you wanted something in life, you had to be willing to take a risk.

The double doors whooshed open as he approached, and he was moving so fast he didn't see the other person coming out until they almost collided. He came up short, but when he raised a hand to apologize to the woman, his heart jumped straight to his throat.

*"Madeline?"* he breathed in utter disbelief.

She was dressed in jeans and a black coat that was much too warm for Texas, with her hair in a messy ponytail and her beautiful face free of makeup except for a splash of pretty pink lipstick. Her golden-brown eyes were wide with the same disbelief that had his own mouth hanging open like trapdoor.

At the exact same time, they both said, "What are you doing here?"

He wanted to grab her and kiss her until neither one of them could breathe, but he had too much to say, and they were still smack-dab in the middle of the doorway, with people streaming in and out all around them.

Grabbing her hand, he tugged her over to the empty bank of couches at one end of the terminal. His heart was hammering against his ribs as he pulled her close and drank in the sight of the woman he'd managed to fall head over heels in love with in a matter of weeks.

Shaking his head, he threaded his fingers with hers and said, "I can't believe you're here. I was just on my way to see you."

Madeline's mouth dropped open as she gaped at him in astonishment. "You were coming to New York City? How? Why?"

He licked his lips and smiled that perfect little crooked smile of his. "Well, there are some things in life that a man needs to say in person. Like I'm sorry—for not being more understanding. And for not being more plain about wanting you to stay. And for not telling you how I really feel."

Stepping closer, he released her hands and looped his arms around her middle, making her stomach dance with butterflies. "Damn it, Maddie, I want you to stay. I figured out I'm destined to love a city girl, and I hope like hell she's willing to love me back."

Everything around them seemed to fade as she gazed into his eyes, overwhelmed and breathless. She shook her head, trying to think of the proper words to describe the joy of hearing him say he loved her, but failing completely.

He hurried on, his expression earnest, his voice sincere. "With all my responsibilities on my grandfather's ranch, I can't move to New York, but if you'd be willing to compromise—and I'm hoping like hell you will be—I'd be willing to move to San Antonio and commute. I know it's not *the* city, but it is *a* city, filled with bustle and noise and all the fancy restaurants you could want."

Tears came to her eyes at his pronouncement. She knew exactly how much Sunnybell meant to him. Offering to move for her was quite possibly the sweetest and most romantic thing anyone had ever done for her.

Blinking back the moisture in her eyes, she shook her head. "Well, I hate to disappoint you, but I'm not moving to San Antonio."

Draping her arms over the back of his neck, she said, "I wasn't back in the city two days before I knew that it didn't feel like home anymore. Come to find out, I prefer horses to taxis after all. I don't know how it happened, but somewhere along the way, my definition of home changed. The city seemed so noisy and impersonal, and all I could think about was the quiet haven I'd found all the way down in Texas…and the man who taught me to enjoy it.

"So, cowboy, I happen to have my heart set on Sunnybell, and on a certain little log cabin with gingham curtains. More than that, I have my heart set on you, Tanner Callen."

He let out a whoop before claiming a kiss hot enough to singe her boots—boots that she had bought to commemorate her decision to move back to Texas. She never imagined she'd fall in love with a cowboy—let alone the small town he lived in—but she knew now that Sunnybell was exactly where she was meant to be.

For the first time ever, she could envision a life that made her happy, not just a life that checked off the boxes on the way to retirement. She never knew what she was missing until she found it and then walked away from it. This time, she was here because she *wanted* to be.

When he finally pulled back from the kiss, he shook his head and looked down at her with love and pride. "So you actually got on a plane for me?"

"I did indeed," she said with a grimace, immensely glad to be on firm ground now. "Once I figured out what I wanted, I didn't want to wait a minute longer to get back to you."

"I like the sound of that," he said, waggling his eyebrows and making her laugh. "What about work? Sunnybell isn't exactly a corporate hotbed."

"I know," she said, since she'd already thought everything through. "But thanks to my parents' insistence that I save 15 percent of every paycheck I earn, I have what I need to chase a silly dream I refused to acknowledge until very recently."

Once the idea had taken hold, she'd not been able to let it go. All of her business training would come in handy, only now she'd be using it for something she actually cared about.

His eyebrows lifted with interest. "And what dream is that?"

"Opening my own little bookstore. Lucky for me, I happen to know a sweet little town with lots of readers and not a single bookstore for miles."

He nodded, admiration shining in his blue-green eyes. "That's the best idea I've heard all day."

"Is it?" she said innocently, fluttering her eyelashes. "Because I have a few other ideas involving the two of us and how we should spend the rest of the day."

His grin was slow and sexy and promised all kinds of delicious things. "Well, darlin', let's get you home, shall we?"

She laughed when he swept her up off her feet, shoulder bag and all. Wrapping her arms around his neck, she sighed and nuzzled in close. "Feels like I'm already there."

## About the Author

ERIN KNIGHTLEY is the *USA Today* bestselling author of a dozen published works, including seven historical romance novels. Initially deciding to pursue a sensible career in science, she eventually came to her senses, leaving her practical side behind in order to write full-time. Together with her tall, dark, and handsome husband, and their three spoiled mutts, she is living her own Happily Ever After in North Carolina.

# Looking to Fall in Love in Just One Night?

## Introducing BookShots Flames:

**original romances presented by James Patterson that fit into your busy life.**

## Featuring Love Stories by:

*New York Times* bestselling author Jen McLaughlin

*New York Times* bestselling author Samantha Towle

*USA Today* bestselling author Erin Knightley

Elizabeth Hayley

Jessica Linden

Codi Gary

Laurie Horowitz

…and many others!

## Available only from

## "ALEX CROSS, I'M COMING FOR YOU...."

Gary Soneji, the killer from *Along Came a Spider,* has been dead for more than ten years—but Cross swears he saw Soneji gun down his partner. Is Cross's worst enemy back from the grave?

Nothing will prepare you for the wicked truth.

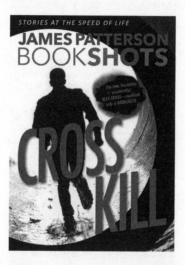

**Read the next riveting, pulse-racing Alex Cross adventure, available only from**

# BOOK**SHOTS**

# WILL THE LAST HUMANS ON EARTH PLEASE TURN OUT THE LIGHTS?

As humans continue to be plagued by vicious animal attacks, zoologist Jackson Oz desperately tries to save the ones he loves—and the rest of mankind. But animals aren't the only threat anymore. Some humans are starting to evolve too, turning into something feral and ferocious....

Could this savage new species save civilization—or end it?

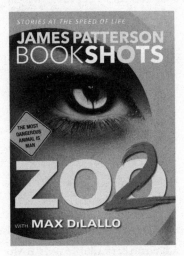

**Read the high-adrenaline page-turner *Zoo II*, available only from**

# BOOK**SHOTS**

## "I'M NOT ON TRIAL. SAN FRANCISCO IS."

Drug cartel boss the Kingfisher has a reputation for being violent and merciless. And after he's finally caught, he's set to stand trial for his vicious crimes—until he begins unleashing chaos and terror upon the lawyers, jurors, and police associated with the case. The city is paralyzed, and Detective Lindsay Boxer is caught in the eye of the storm.

Will the Women's Murder Club make it out alive—or will a sudden courtroom snare ensure their last breaths?

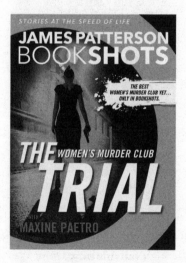

**Read the shocking new Women's Murder Club story,**
available now from

# BOOK**SHOTS**

## SOME GAMES AREN'T FOR CHILDREN....

After a nasty divorce, Christy Moore finds her escape in Marty Hawking, who introduces her to all sorts of new experiences, including an explosive new game called "Make-Believe."

But what begins as innocent fun soon turns dark, and as Marty pushes the boundaries further and further, the game may just end up deadly.

**Read the white-knuckle thriller, coming soon from**

# BOOK**SHOTS**

## MICHAEL BENNETT FACES HIS TOUGHEST CASE YET....

Detective Michael Bennett is called to the scene after a man plunges to his death outside a trendy Manhattan hotel—but the man's fingerprints are traced to a pilot who was killed in Iraq years ago.

Will Bennett discover the truth?

Or will he become tangled in a web of government secrets?

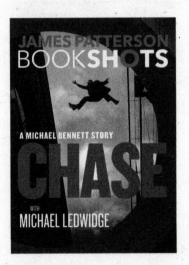

**Read the new action-packed Michael Bennett story, *Chase*, coming soon from**

# BOOK**SHOTS**